CRACKS IN THE IMAGE

CRACKS

STORIES BY

THE

GAY MEN

EDITED BY

IN

RICHARD DIPPLE

IMAGE

GAY MEN'S PRESS

First published 1981 by Gay Men's Press,
P O Box 247, London N15 6RW, England.
Second impression November 1982.
Edited by Richard Dipple
World copyright on the collection © Gay Men's Press 1981;
each individual work © the author 1981.

British Library Cataloguing in Publication Data

Cracks in the image.
  1. Short stories, English
  I. Burt, Simon
  823'.01'08[FS]   PR1309.S5

ISBN 0 907040 08 X

Cover and design by Aubrey Walter
Photoset by Shanta Thawani, 25 Natal Road, London N11 2NU
Printed and bound by A. Wheaton and Co. Ltd., Exeter

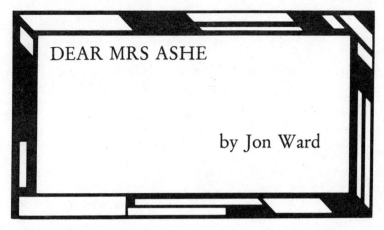

DEAR MRS ASHE

by Jon Ward

I'll have one more go.

> Queen's Avenue,
> W.3.
> 19th April

> Dear Mrs Ashe,
>   Since Thursday morning's meeting with the
> police, I have become increasingly concerned
> about my position. I feel the decision-making
> processes adopted revealed scant regard for
> elementary justice. I am well apprised of the
> social and personality factors involved. Surely,
> though, it is the court, not our department,
> which must ascertain whether Michael Ríos
> removed the tyres from Father Randolph's
> dormobile. Until then, the boy's proper home is
> with his mother, and I can only regard as
> premature any

Gavin! For crying out loud . . . I suppose my fantasies are no less
scratched and dated than Gavin's, but at least I don't amplify them
all over the house. How am I meant to write to Mrs Ashe with a
dead rock artist richocheting about the room?

> Dear Mrs Ashe,
>   Close your mind and open your veins,
>   We gotta burn —

It occurs to me that a lot of Gavin's performance must be an
appeal of some kind. But to whom? Piers and the others assume
he's 'my' friend. Which is quite unfair. Gavin only moved into the

little bedsit beneath my room a couple of months ago. And whenever he comes upstairs, it's invariably Piers he talks to. At, rather. Poor Gavin — all he ever wants is to share the unpublished secrets of Eddie Lawn's Alabama schooldays, or lend us old Crush records. As if we haven't heard them through the floor already. Piers, of course, can't abide all that vulgar hero-worship.

'He died in his bath. Of aspirin poisoning. Don't you think it's terrible?' Gavin says, standing woodenly in our little hallway. His bus conductor's uniform and rather sturdy frame have an unsettling effect on the three Malevich reproductions carefully pasted over our telephone table. Piers giggles.

'Well, yes, it's dreadful,' he agrees, his skeletal shoulders shaking a little inside a baggy maroon cardigan.

Gavin is immune to irony. He continues to stare at Piers with those moist, wide eyes. 'He once said about Crush "Think of us as erotic guerillas." Isn't that amazing?'

Piers' smile fades. Of all the qualities that have enthralled me since I first sat on the Peruvian rug in his college room and listened to him extemporise on the mystery of rhyme, it is his stubbornness, subtle but extreme, that stands out. Piers' intellectual integrity is completely democratic. He makes no allowance for feeling, age or social class. Recalling some bizarre encounter in the ironmonger's, he will explain rather primly 'Things were said that could *not* be allowed to pass.' Eddie Lawn's messianic claims are clearly not allowed to pass.

'I'm not sure that means anything, you know.' As he leans against the door of his room, Piers' gaze drifts above Gavin's dishevelled fair curls. 'Sexual protest, I suspect, always dissolves its own effects. That was the Reichian error.' The smile returns through his new dark beard. ' "Erotic gurrilla",' he muses, 'don't you think it's rather *passé?*'

The morning I met Piers at Trinity, I had shyly placed some poems of mine in his hands, like a bowl of rice at the foot of a stone buddha. He read them back to me straight away. His voice, softly precise as a swallow's wings, rose and fell through my lines to stunning effect. 'Interesting,' he remarked when he'd given them back to me. It was, I came to learn, the highest accolade. He complemented at once with his most mortal censure: 'But a little *passé.*' It may be because I am uncommonly quick in response to such delicate admonitions — my very next poems were simply 'interesting' — that Piers gathered me up when he left university and settled me here in the spare room of his London flat.

Gavin, by contrast, is impenetrable. He refuses to budge under

Piers' quiet assault. His normally pale, unlined face flushes pink, and the trace of Leicester in his voice becomes more audible.

'No, no,' he insists, 'it's Eddie Lawn. You know, Crush. It's more than music. It's a way of life. You should listen some time.'

I've been hovering silently in the half-open doorway of my room. I know that at this point, Piers will imperceptibly edge Gavin in my direction and retire to the kitchen. But why do I, too, sense that it was not to Piers Gavin wanted to retell the story of his idol's last ablutions? It must be my training in psychopathology. Everything's a little bit twisted.

> Queen's Avenue,
> W.3.
> 22nd April

Dear Mrs Ashe,
    I feel I have reached a point in my life when I need to reconsider my directions. It is not easy, I assure you, to establish

How cumbersome my explanations are. Piers never explains himself — only his ideas. I'm afraid that's something I couldn't sustain. I can talk to Gavin, oddly enough. Things clarify. Not that he often comes into my room. His visits usually terminate in the hallway, as if he were a tradesman politely being humoured while somebody counts the change. Only when he crosses an indefinable boundary, perhaps a threshold of tolerance, is he ushered into my company. For it is always Piers who fixes this point. And while Piers' discreet amusement embarrasses me — for might I not be guilty, by association, of some unconscious absurdity akin to Gavin's? — I look forward to these rare visits. There's an excitement about Gavin's presence (not unmixed with discomfort) which I find hard to specify, but which I always recognise immediately. I've sometimes simply put it down to his build. His body seems to press through that shabby costume and disrupt the unfinished attempts at aesthetic living (obliquely copied from Piers) which furnish my room. And then the room seems so small: with Gavin here, I literally don't know where to put myself. I shuffle about, picking papers up, folding clothes away, mutely drawing attention to this or that ornament or book or photograph; and all the time, my movements seem to me afflicted with a sort of gaucheness, as if my joints were audibly clicking, or my limbs kept fetching up in slightly the wrong space. Yet the easy gaze which follows me about is void of accusation.

Gavin gives to my chatter — of which he manages to trigger a veritable outpouring — the most unwavering attention. His own speech, when it comes, is something else. Gavin's words are things. He doesn't converse. Simple announcements, often comically abrupt, punctuate his watchful silence.

'I steal all my food,' he told me, à propos of nothing I had said, a couple of weeks ago. It transpired he is saving up for a pilgrimage to the States. His goal is the outdoor stadium in Pittsburgh where Eddie Lawn was arrested on stage for indecent exposure. Perched on the edge of my bed, Gavin spoke emphatically, his strong legs wide apart, his pale hands clasped tightly in front of him.

'He was *completely* misunderstood.'

Considering his allegiances, Gavin is surprisingly lenient about my profession. I sometimes suspect he admires me for it. He certainly enjoys my stories about the department. This attention lends a temporary but warming sense of substance to my working life. It was satisfying to counter Gavin's morbid compassion for his deceased hero by telling him about the day I met Annie McEwen. Annie is the mother of young Michael Ríos, and one of the clients Mrs Ashe hung on to — as a souvenir of real life I suppose — when she took over the department. (Mrs Ashe doesn't like teenagers, so she gave Michael to me.) That Friday afternoon, Mrs Ashe was in Southend, addressing a conference on The Caring Community, and I was dispatched into reception to calm Annie down. There were three or four middle-aged women hunched in foam armchairs against the khaki walls. I guessed at once which was the famous Annie from her grubby pink mackintosh and incongruously new wooden clogs.

'Mrs McEwen?' I asked soothingly. She ignored this, so I walked right up to her. She stared ahead, her thin face blotched with crying, her hair both stiff and straggly.

'Mrs McEwen,' I said again. She lifted her face.

'Who've they sent me? A juvenile *delinquent?*' Her Scots voice was astonishingly powerful.

'Would you like to come this way?' I adopted a firm, grown-up manner. Mrs McEwen stumbled to her feet and began to sob.

'Where's Mrs Ashe?'

'I'm afraid —'

'I'm going back to see Father Randolph. *He* understands me.' She made slowly for the exit. I glanced round the room, and met the unfriendly stares of the other women.

'Why don't we talk about it in here?' I pointed invitingly to one of the little windowless cells where interviews are conducted.

Annie turned and looked at me.

'Oh, what the hell.' She wiped her nose on the back of her hand and followed me in. I spent the next hour trying to dissuade Annie from returning to her twelfth-floor flat and jumping out of the window. It wasn't her flat anymore, I explained. I'd read the file: Annie hadn't paid her rent for nine months. Now Michael had run away back to his father, she was no longer an unsupported mother. So we couldn't stop the council taking the flat back. On top of that, if Michael returned he'd find her homeless, and probably have to go into care. Annie McEwen may be histrionic, but she's no fool. None of my non-commital optimism could shift the logic of her argument. If she had to leave her flat, it might as well be through the window. The deadlock was broken with appropriate drama. Mrs Ashe appeared. She was a little out of breath, but no less resplendent in coral necklace and expensive sea-green slacks. And on her heels, as if he, too, had been addressing the Southend conference, Michael Ríos sauntered in. Annie by now had broken out of the interviewing room. She pointed to her young son propped expressionless against the waiting-room radiator, and shouted at Mrs Ashe:

'Would you like to be in my shoes?'

Mrs Ashe said brightly, 'I expect I'd manage somehow.'

'Well try, then!' Annie cried. She took off her new clogs and threw them at Mrs Ashe, first one, then the other.

'A danger to herself and others,' Mrs Ashe announced hotly as she strode into the receptionist's cubicle to phone for a GP. And Annie McEwen was locked up in St Cuthbert's for the weekend.

I finished telling this story with my back to Gavin, staring out of the window. I was uncomfortably aware that he was standing very close behind me, gazing over my shoulder at the inert terrace opposite. He wanted to know about Michael — but what could I say? At fifteen, not very tall, in his skimpy purple sweater and cheap school trousers, there is about Michael Ríos an immediate suggestion of nudity. I suppose it's a matter of complexion, though my interest has always been too cautious to permit a very exact observation. Not, I'm sure, that Michael minds being looked at. I remember reading (was it in *Stages of Normal Adolescence* or Tawny's *Adolescent Pathology*? I always did get them confused) how teenage boys often display greater narcissism than teenage girls. Even against the barrack-room decor of Area 3 reception, Michael managed to remain, through all the mayhem, immaculately casual. For a moment long enough to be uncomfortable, I quite forgot what I was there for.

So I answered Gavin's enquiry as simply as I could.

'Michael didn't say a word,' I told him. 'He slipped out of the building and wasn't seen again until the police nicked him for stealing Father Randolph's tyres.' I turned to face Gavin as he made slowly for the door. Hesitating, he stared all around my room — at the unfinished letters of resignation, at the rubber plant which has died next to my typewriter, at the Antonioni stills uneasily taped over the gas fire — then he said something rather odd:

'You should spend more money on clothes.'

Why does it matter *what* I write to Mrs Ashe? The short answer to that is Piers. Ever since I met him, I have been a slave to words — worse, the *right* words. Piers casts a spell of language on everything and everyone he approaches. It permeates his room, that rare, abstract force — it's in the familiar Peruvian rug, in his exquisite ferns, in the lines of Heine thoughtfully inscribed back to front round the goldfish bowl on his desk.

'But *really*,' Piers giggles from behind his Montaigne, '*social* work.' If I'd never heard 'social work' pronounced in quite that way, I probably wouldn't be writing to Mrs Ashe at all.

All right then. What would Piers say? He'd probably alarm her with a quotation.

> Dear Mrs Ashe,
>   *qué nocturno rumor, qué muerta blanca!*

or

> Dear Mrs Ashe,
>   This honey is delicious
>   *But it burns the throat*

Well — if Piers is no help, at least I don't have to contend with Eddie Lawn this evening. Gavin's been out a lot recently. He's very cagey about it. I ran into him in the downstairs hall a couple of nights ago. I was going for one of those late walks that can sometimes lend one's life a spurious gloss of romance. Gavin had just come in. Or had he just shown someone out? He was very peculiar, either way. He was flushed, and he laughed when he saw me. I asked him where he'd been.

'Night buses.' He laughed again. He was wearing a rather strange get-up: all black, apparently all the same synthetic material. Maybe he was just very stoned. He invited me into his room, and when I declined, he peered at me and smiled and shook

his head. I couldn't smile back, but neither could I move. I stood
in front of him, feeling exposed and a little awkward. His face,
very close to mine, was all at once possessed of an intense
seriousness — eyes unblinking, lips a little apart. He raised his
hands and placed them on my shoulders. The full weight of him
seemed to sink into me. Something inside me began to shift and
crumble, like old brickwork exposed to a new stress. Then he
dropped his hands, turned, and disappeared into his room. I
lingered in the hall a minute. From Gavin's room, I heard the
rattle and click of a record going on to a turntable. The prospect
of Eddie Lawn shook me from my reverie. I headed quickly for the
front door. Before I could reach it, the air about me trembled with
the unmistakable, sweet rapid notes of a jazz saxophone. I was
more than startled. Whatever Gavin had dislodged within me
broke clean away: I was seized with an irresistible urge to cry. Very
frightened, I bolted back upstairs to my room, and put myself to
bed.

If I don't finish this letter this evening, I shall die an assistant
director of Newham Social Services.

Queen's Avenue,
W.3.
May 2nd

Dear Mrs Ashe,

Dammit. I'm worrying about Gavin again. I've been down
twice this evening already. He's just shaken, that's all. He had a
terrible time last night and he's still a bit upset. He's not going to
die or anything.

Dear Mrs Ashe,

I still don't know why they came. Gavin insists it has nothing to
do with his shoplifting antics.
'They were looking for someone. They won't come back.' He
had trouble talking because his mouth was bruised. I've never seen
Gavin angry before. 'Bastards! Bastards!' he kept saying, while I
was trying to get him to lie down and sip some hastily improvised
tea.
I'd been upstairs in Piers' room when they arrived. Piers was
unusually pleased with himself. He was putting the finishing
touches to a joint he'd been rolling on a library copy of

Heidegger's *Being and Time*. A thin young woman, whose name I still don't know, knelt next to his expensive cane chair, staring bleakly at an oboe case on the floor in front of her.

'I've just invented a new literary movement,' Piers giggled. 'The Ipthilimists.'

'Ipthilimists?' I enquired.

'Ipthilimism,' Piers explained, 'is the pursuit of the perfect sentence. Everything an Ipthilimist writes may be regarded as a cypher which can only be broken by the message it carries. Formally speaking, Ipthilimism could be said to occupy a white space surrounded by an ever increasing mass of language. Interesting, isn't it?' Piers chuckled, and looked first at me, then at his mute companion.

'But what *is* the perfect sentence?' I wanted to know.

'Oh, it's unutterable!' Piers retorted. 'I wrote my first Ipthilimist poem today. Do you want to hear it? It's called "Binary Star".' He giggled again. 'Of course.'

Piers' friend took Heidegger from him without looking up. As he bent over his desk, I asked:

'Why Ipthilimism? I don't get the etymology.'

'Ipthilimel —' Piers paused '— was a nun. I discovered her today in a monograph on Ramus. She attempted to construct a *wholly linguistic* alchemy. Can you believe it? She was burned at the stake in 1311.'

Piers found his poem.

'Binary Star,' he began, in his light, emphatic voice.

I thought the frosted glass in the front door downstairs was going to disintegrate. The hammering went on for a full minute, all but smothering the rhythmic bellow of 'Police! Police!' At last we heard Gavin walk down the hall and open the door. The cacophony ceased, or rather it changed into an indecipherable roar of masculine voices.

'Oh dear, dear,' Piers whispered, still clutching his unread poem. With surprising alacrity, his friend opened her oboe case and swept clean the book she was holding. Below us, the torrent of speech suddenly broke into a raucous, locker-room laugh. For the first time, we heard Gavin's voice, strained and irate, rising above the rest.

'The word is *gay!*'

There was a moment's silence, then a flurry of shuffles and bumps. The front door slammed, and there was silence again. It was broken at length by Gavin's uncertain footsteps as he made his way back to his room. The young woman and I looked instinctively at Piers.

'No, no,' he murmured, and smiled. 'The word is *Ipthilimist*.'

'Piers —' I began, but I was trembling too much to continue. I managed to seize hold of the oboe case, though, and take out the finished joint. Crossing the room shakily, I closed Piers' door behind me, and ran downstairs.

> The Small Cats,
> Bleeker Street,
> Greenwich Village.
> 20th May

Mrs Ashe, dear,

I'm in New York. I'm in love. I won't be back. Next stop Pittsburgh. Maybe not Pittsburgh. Maybe L.A. I'll let you have the address, whichever, so you can forward my last pay cheque.

Oh and would you do me a favour? Take proper care of little Michael Ríos.

> Bye,

AN INEXACT PARALLEL

by Peter Robins

'This your first teaching post then?'

'Not the rosiest of beginnings, is it?'

'Unfortunate, let's say. You'll be staying on though?'

'Just after five this morning I'd decided to resign immediately. I had a letter yesterday from a college friend who's lecturing in East Africa. Something could be found for me out there as well almost immediately, if I want it.'

'You know, Mr Griffith, in our experience it's best not to scamper off after an incident like this. Let the stink blow away. Shows you align yourself with the school rather than with the gentleman concerned — if you take my meaning, sir.'

'If I hadn't worked that out for myself I would hardly have dragged you from your breakfast, Inspector.'

'All in a morning's work, Mr Griffith. Now, if you wouldn't mind winding up the window on your side, I'll read this statement back to you and perhaps you'd be good enough to sign it.'

Alan glanced at the rain, spattering across a muddy backwater of the canal. For the thirtieth time in as many hours he damned Molesbridge School. What was it, anyway, but a twilight zone of the teaching world? He damned the snivelling thirteen-year-old Cogginson who had less charm than a drenched white rat. He damned the arrogant and predatory Headmaster. Most of all, he damned himself. Molesbridge could have been an unnoticed advertisement in a journal barely glanced at on a plane bound for Africa, three thousand sunny miles south. Had he only said yes to Janet instead of prevaricating he'd not have submerged himself in a prim market town on the edge of living.

The Inspector's voice intruded, trudging its factual path through the happenings of the previous evening.

'. . . having concluded my rehearsal for the school's forthcoming production of *Julius Caesar*, I returned to the Staff Common

Room, collected my case and umbrella and made my way through the playing fields in the direction of the bus stop. The Market Hall clock was striking eight. Correct so far, Mr Griffith?'

'Correct, Inspector.'

'At the gate leading into Orchard Lane I was stopped by my House Captain, James Struthern, aged seventeen. He informed me that he had received a complaint from Ronald Cogginson, a thirteen-year-old pupil. This complaint took the form of a serious allegation against the Headmaster of Molesbridge School, the Reverend Dr Simpson Benedict M.A. The boy Cogginson, who was stated to be in some distress, insisted that the Headmaster, during the course of giving private instruction on tying scout knots, had interfered with him. This interference was of a sexual nature. The Headmaster's right hand had been placed first on the boy's thigh outside his shorts and, subsequently, inside. There had been some handling of the boy's genitals resulting in a stiffening of the penis. No climax had been reached since the Headmaster's activities had been interrupted by his wife knocking at the door. The boy Cogginson had not resisted the Headmaster's advances, being in a state of some confusion and fear. Still an accurate record of the facts, Mr Griffith?'

'As far as we have them, Inspector.'

'Quite. Not much more, sir . . . My House Captain, James Struthern, also about to leave the school after play rehearsal, had discovered Cogginson crying in the locker room. The boy gave his story as outlined and Struthern repeated it to me.'

And asked me, Alan added to himself, what I intended to do about the incident. There had seemed to be three options which he had listed to the stolid, already pompous sixth-former as they had faced one another by the school gate. Both boys — Cogginson and Struthern — might have gone with him to confront the Headmaster. There would have been an apocalyptic scene with possible further outcrops of the violence which both staff and boys had noted in Simpson Benedict when he was crossed or thwarted. That would have resolved nothing. Secondly, Alan had temporised, he himself might do nothing. Struthern had been ready for that. Reared in a family that measured Christianity by the frequency of church attendance, his reply was well-seasoned with self-righteousness. 'If you don't take any action, sir, the prefects would interpret it as condoning the Headmaster's behaviour. It might, with respect, put a question mark against your own professional standards, Mr Griffith.' That had stung. To be measured against Simpson Benedict was infuriating. What had Alan Griffith in common with a self-indulgent clown who relished fingering pubescent boys? His own involvement throughout college with Janet was a galaxy removed from Simpson Benedict's sticky little indiscretions.

'. . . if you haven't brought your own pen, Mr Griffith, you can use mine.'

'What do you think he'll get, Inspector?'

'Depends, sir. If it were just this boy, er, Cogginson, defence might swing probation with a stipulation that he leave teaching and see a psychiatrist regularly. Not that it ever does much good. He won't starve though. I don't doubt a chaplaincy will be fixed somewhere abroad for him. He'll be able to make a fresh start — in more senses than one, more than likely. Africa perhaps — the Mediterranean coast might suit him. Would that be the part where your friend is working, Mr Griffith?'

Whether the remark was unpremeditated, Alan couldn't know. It altered his estimate of the Inspector. The man was suddenly less predictable; more disturbing.

'Janet is in East Africa, Inspector. Tell me, why did you say "just this boy Cogginson"?'

'I'm fifty-two, Mr Griffith. Molesbridge isn't the first case of this kind to drop on my desk. Nor the last, I'd say. But I wouldn't give long odds on Cogginson being the only boy involved. There'll be another half-dozen come forward to you by the end of the week. Two will be telling the truth — sufficient to clinch our case. The rest will be bursting with adolescent fantasies and a lust for notoriety. They're the dangerous ones. Home Office would crucify us if we slipped on a delicate business like this, let alone the media. I know damn fine he did it, Mr Griffith, but our friend Simpson Benedict has heavyweight friends and relatives in *Who's Who*. One brother's an Air Commodore; another's a Life Peer. If he thinks there's an outside chance of an acquittal, I'll be sparring with a top QC rearing to clear the family name.'

'And if he doesn't get away with it?'

'Evens on fifteen months with good behaviour. He'll need that dog-collar inside, you know. Your average villain doesn't rate a child-fancier. Always tickles me the way the real hard cases become virtuous about sex. A fair few of them were on the game themselves in their teens. No, Mr Griffith. Forget Simpson Benedict. He'll get his chaplaincy somewhere with better weather than this when he's out. No justice is there? Now I'll not keep you. Just bring this lad Cogginson as far as the Orchard Gate after lunch will you? If you point him in the direction of the car, I'll be standing quite handy here at the corner and we'll take over from there.'

Alan hurried back along the soggy Berkshire lane to take his one remaining lesson of the morning. As he walked into the Lower Sixth form room, he knew that they knew. Despite promises exacted from Cogginson and, more importantly, from Struthern, they all knew. The sum of their speculation patterned the silence as he made for his desk.

'Shall we continue with *Julius Caesar?*' Struthern asked.

'We can't. There's no Brutus. Jones is sick again,' another chirped.

Upton, the quiet one, as neat in his build as in his choice of shirts and his handling of a cricket bat, looked Alan coolly in the face and said, 'You could read Brutus, couldn't you, Mr Griffith?'

Alan knew then that they were certain he had already contacted the police. Not that I loved Simpson Benedict less, but that I loved Molesbridge more. An inexact parallel. Whatever might have tortured Brutus in his orchard, Alan detested Simpson Benedict for the scandal in which he was about to drench them all and, far from loving it, he didn't give more than half a damn for Molesbridge School.

'We'll leave *Julius Caesar* for the moment,' he announced. 'I did ask you all to look through *Nicholas Nickleby* last weekend with particular reference to Victorian education of the poor. Now you can write one side only on just that. If there's time before lunch, we might discuss it.'

As they began to write, Alan stared at the twenty heads in front of him. A random sample of seventeen-year-olds. Where would they be in ten years? Assistants in banks maybe, laced to a girl from the school across the canal by two kids and a mortgage. Two or three might make salesmen, speeding south at weekends in the company car, intent on dining and bedding the office secretary. Could it matter to any of them that Simpson Benedict was removed or that he stayed on to maul more third-formers? It was the question that had cost Alan more than a pack of cigarettes and a night's sleep. Yet he was sure, without priggishness, that his decision to ring the CID had been the utilitarian's choice, whatever the opinion of the prefects. Precisely because the twenty whispering teenagers in front of him would never climb Everest or write musicals or play for England, their school would be one of the few landmarks in their unexceptional lives. Some ulcerous, some bald, some alcoholic, they would all think back, even come back, to Molesbridge. To ensure that their reference to it did not provoke a saloon-bar snigger, Simpson Benedict had to go.

Twice Alan glanced towards the window. Beyond the muddy footpaths, the canal and cheerless Berkshire, to the south-east there was sunlight, Africa and Janet. Without further consideration of the priorities involved: Janet or sunshine, Janet and sunshine, he began to word a cable. Whenever he looked up after crossing out a word, he was aware that Upton was looking at him with that frank hazel stare.

'You'll not find the answer printed on my face Upton.'

'You want to watch Upton, sir.'

'Upton's going to be a porn king, sir.'

'Just shows what a sewer you've got in your head. It's all because I told them I want to be a photographer, sir.'

'Shut up all of you and scribble.'

On the stairs to the Common Room for lunch, Alan was stopped by his House Captain. Struthern asked if there had been any developments. Alan indicated that the matter was no longer in his hands and that it was fortunate the incident had occurred so near the end of term. It was probable that Molesbridge would have a new Headmaster for the summer. He asked Struthern to ensure that Cogginson went to the Orchard Gate immediately after lunch. 'And, Struthern,' he added, 'you'll make a good politician, even if it is only in some tatty office. Despite the promise I asked for last night, it's very plain you've discussed the situation with sufficient sixth-formers to pressure me into action: a presupposition I find insulting.'

He did not care for Struthern and was delighted that the boy would be leaving within months. More imagination would be needed in settling on a new House Captain. Upton, he thought, might be pleasant to work with. There was a tough honesty about the lad for, like Alan himself, Upton came from an unpretentious home, his father a boat-builder who had made good.

It was as he turned from giving the snivelling Cogginson a shove in the direction of the War Memorial, where he could see the Inspector lighting a cigarette, that Alan noticed Upton idling near the cricket pavilion. An opportune moment, he thought, to chat and find out what made the lad tick.

Upton, as it happened, spoke first.

'Sir? Might I have a word?'

'Surely. We'd best walk back towards the school. There'll be another downpour within minutes.'

'About Cogginson, Mr Griffith.'

Alan was immediately impatient, wanting to talk about summer

and to regard Cogginson and Simpson Benedict as finite yester-
days. It was impossible, he conceded ruefully. The probings and
gossip, the trial, jokes and press reports would reverberate for
months, echoing against the edges of every conversation.

'What about him?'

'Can I speak freely? Sort of off-the-record as the politicians say?'

'Just get on with it. I'm already shattered by the whole sordid
business.'

'I was thinking only this morning, it can't have been easy for
you. Wouldn't have been for any of us, well — me anyway . . . '

'Upton . . . '

'Sorry. Well, I'm not sure if it's relevant but Cogginson isn't
exactly a virgin you know. Ever since last autumn he's been doing
things for three or four of us that I suppose, well, that we ought to
have been doing for ourselves. Nothing heavy, like oral or anal.
And not for money, of course. I think he enjoys doing it, if you see
what I'm getting at.'

Alan stopped; turned to face the teenager who was as tall as
himself. He looked beyond the freckled face towards the south
where unbroken cloudbanks had begun to dwindle. And then he
shouted: 'What am I bloody into? Blast you, Upton; blast that
little trollop Cogginson and blast Molesbridge. This place is
becoming a mudbath and I wish to Christ I was out of it. Look.
Here. Go on; look. This is Janet. I should have gone to Africa with
her or, anyway, I should never have come here.'

'She's quite photogenic. Do her freckles get worse in the
summer? Mine do.'

'I don't know, Upton, but if I could walk out of here this
afternoon I'd bloody soon find out. You realise that's what I'd like
to do — never set eyes on any of you again?'

'I hope you don't. If it makes any odds at all, I'd miss you more
than a bit,' Upton said and then, not looking away, winked.

Alan felt that his feet were losing their grip, that he could no
longer control his balance on the muddy path. He glanced away
from Upton hastily, seeking some certainty in Janet's smile. In a
world where he was winked at by seventeen-year-olds, at least
Janet's grey glance was an assurance of stability. Only as he
looked, really looked at the photograph, did he realise her eyes
were not grey but, like Upton's, hazel.

BECALMED

by Barry Nonweiler

We struggled out of the bush and came upon the lake at last, my shoulders aching from carrying so much weight in the inappropriate bag I had brought with me; Rawiri pointed excitedly ahead at the gable of a wooden roof, just visible through the trees beyond a stretch of cleared land, and said 'Hey, Peter, we're there!' I had listened so often to Rawiri calling up from his memory the old family bach, all through two winters, when we lay stretched out beside one another on the carpet in the glow of the fire, while outside the wind sighed endlessly, that I thought I would have recognised it myself at once, or at least found the place familiar; but I did not.

Every time it seemed I had come close to you, I had not been where I thought I was.

Bewildered, I stood behind Rawiri in the shade and stared. Rawiri gave a child-like cry and flung up his arms, the half-caste skin of his hands flashing golden in the sunlight, and ran helterskelter down the green slope ahead, his faded satchel bobbing up and down beneath his tousled black hair, cumbrously graceful like an animal in his boots, even when he stumbled. Soon he was a long way from me.

So many times I had thought, now you and I will be completely together: so many times everything, after all, had remained as before. And even now, I thought it must be this time. Now that we had finally got here, to the bach, even if we had only managed two days off work at the same time.

So much of our lives is shaped by unreal expectations of the world, so much of our histories becomes a long sequence of disillusion. We find ourselves forced to struggle with our dreams. They become as much enemies to our fulfilment as our oppressors. We live in dark times.

I followed Rawiri across the uneven pasture, slowly, because I was tired. I had not slept well the night before, though I told Rawiri that I had. I felt desperately uncomfortable staying with his twin brother, Anaru, and his trim Dutch wife, in that immaculate house with its picture-window views and thermal pool. Anaru had become everything their foster-parents might have wanted of him: he had settled in his home town, become a successful solicitor, married a pakeha wife, owned his own house in a large and enviable section. The dreams of a philanthropic judge, who had died while his foster-sons were quite young, but whose iron grip of kindness had never set either of them free.

Not either of them. In fact, I had first met Rawiri at university. I was part-time, and he was full-time then, but we ended up in the same English tutorial. At that time, he seemed to me almost like a wolf-boy, his small body twisting restlessly within the cramped pretentiously respectable clothes that his foster-father would have liked to know he was wearing, his eyes vast and baleful, pacing to and fro in their sockets. And yet his hands, with their stubby fingers and bitten dirty nails, always held the book with that kind of gentle caring respect with which he approached other human beings. I felt almost flattered when he first spoke to me, that soft little breeze of speech, like the kindly movement of a warm spring day, with his characteristic quiet joy speaking through his humbly admitted perplexity at life.

He had left university at the end of that year. By then we were already close friends. He worked first at the freezing-works for a season, and then became a bus driver, which seemed to suit his nomadic temperament. He was radiant, but always just beyond the radiance, like wolves drawn to a camp-fire, there prowled his guilt at not living up to his foster-father's expectations, even though the man had by then been dead for years.

It was their foster-mother who had kept alive the names the children had been given by their biological mother, except when talking to her husband. He always used the English equivalents, except on official documents.

How unlike Rawiri Anaru looked, with his neatly clipped moustache, staring out at me resentfully from his suit. The two of them, Anaru and his wife, made me feel dirty and clumsy. Somehow Rawiri never looked clumsy.

When I got to the bach, the door was already open, and Rawiri was inside. Almost nervous, I stood for a moment, in the heavy calm of the warm bright morning, listening to the bush. There was a sweet chemical smell in the air, as if of something cooking, the smell of thermal activity. A grey warbler was singing nearby, the same song over and over again, launching out fresh and expectant but then pausing, and falling away in a slow descending scale, in which every note was repeated as if to emphasise the regret.

'Hey, aren't you coming in?' called Rawiri through the wall.

He showed me around with the excited pride of a child, pointing to faded photographs, pieces of old furniture, fishing rods, all of which I knew as if from a history book. It was still strange for me to find myself in what was after all no more than a wooden cabin, with no electricity and its own water-tank. It was threatened by a kind of fairy-tale unreality, which I wanted to deny. I didn't want to escape here, I wanted to grow here. I wanted to put my arms around you; but I never did. I always waited until you held me.

Which you did, of course, now and then. The rareness, the unexpectedness of that gentle touch made it seem unimaginably kind. The touch of your kindness bruised me, gripped me fast, unable ever to break free.

'Let's go and pick some blackberries while the sun's here, Pete,' said Rawiri, energetically pulling off the bush-shirt he had taken to wearing only recently. His boots and socks were already lying where he had thrown them, one battered boot on its side as if wounded, the socks a tiny crumpled whirl. The shirt rose jerkily from the unselfconscious lines of his body, and then the flash of his smile, the wiry black hair only looking the more luxuriant for its ruffling. 'It's hot, eh? I can show you around outside while we're at it. How's that?'

I shrugged, and smiled agreement. As usual. 'Sounds good.' Tentatively, I took off my shoes, and my jacket. After all these years, I still found it hard to get used to a climate that was kindly enough to be able to go without clothes. It still felt the very reverse of natural. And so I kept my shirt on, unbuttoning the chest a bit.

When I first came here, I suppose I dreamt of little less than a new order. I would leave the dark of the poverty-stricken industrial port where I had struggled to grow up, pale and stilted: and enter the sun. I was young, it struck me like that. Naively, I believed that what I was trying to escape was a country, and not a system. I had my trade as a printer, and my flat looking out over the harbour. Perhaps if I had not had my expectations, perhaps if I had not been gay, I would never have noticed what was really going on about me, what I was still trapped in, after all. What if the difference between rich and poor was not so obvious? That only confirms the fact that the system must be insidious to survive.

Anyway, it is impossible not to see the difference between a white face and a brown one.

I had thought I could find justice and kindness, in a land of plenty. How beautifully I dreamt! These were some dreams that were indeed the reflection of our suppressed deepest needs.

When I met you, with your brooding ideals and your clear-sighted marxist friends, it was as if the muddled jigsaw-pieces of my perceptions had been put together for me.

I was very grateful. I had few friends then, all of them straight, and although I spent a lot of time with them — in the pub, having a barbecue, the usual things — they brought me little joy and less strength, and even less knowledge. Sexually, I lived among the debris of what I thought a hopelessly confused past, which I kept trying to sweep into a corner and ignore: Rawiri was not so much a clean broom as a whole new living space.

Because the order between you and me seemed to be based on equity and kindness. Back in the north of England, in my late teens and early twenties, every aborted fragment of a relationship had been based on power; at first the power of another over me, and then in reaction, my power over another. You and I shared.

The moment we stepped outside the bach, the ambiguous thermal smell struck me again, and I inhaled it nostalgically. It was already associated indelibly with the enchantment that this frightening beautiful part of the land had for me, this forested heart of the country, continually shifting and transforming itself, half-hidden in aromatic drifts of steam.

'Where does the smell come from?' I asked Rawiri.

He shrugged. 'There must be something rotting,' he said, 'a dead bird perhaps.'

'I thought it was a thermal smell.'

'No, you can't smell that here,' he called back, disappearing up the track through the bush.

I stood for a moment. Then I followed him, and found him at the top of the small hill, leaning against a pohutukawa growing on the steep edge that fell away to the water, looking out over the curving stretch of the lake, turquoise in the sunshine. The air shimmered with the interleaving sound of cicadas.

'No one can see us up here,' he said, hearing me approach, but not turning to look. 'I'm going to take all my clothes off.' He unzipped his jeans, and stepped easily out of them without losing his balance, flinging them carelessly over a branch of the pohutukawa.

His skin was dappled gold and black by the bars of sun and

shade beneath the tree, as if he were camouflaged, and as he turned and stepped gracefully towards me, his feet falling as if trying not to bruise the earth, his dark eyes crouched and alert within their great white caves, he seemed a forest creature. Naked, in the full sunlight, with the green sprawling all around, he was a human being after all, but one who belonged to this earth, for whom and in whom nature luxuriated. As he came towards me I felt myself dwindle and shrink, a piece of industrial refuse lying inappropriately in the bush. In my country there had not even been any land to belong to.

In silence, he leant over and picked some blackberries off a bramble beside me, crushing some into his mouth, holding the others out to me in his already stained hand. 'We wouldn't have blackberries if the pakeha hadn't brought them, eh?' he said, smiling, the juice running between his teeth.

'At least they didn't quite overrun the country, like the gorse,' I said, 'and the pakehas.'

When we had filled an empty ice-cream container with blackberries, we took them back to the bach. I was afraid to speak to you, because I wanted to. You were afraid of involvement, because you wanted it; or so I thought.

I was going to put my shirt back on, because I was bothered by sandflies who seemed to single me out, but Rawiri said we should go for a swim while it was still warm. I dawdled after him to the edge of the lake, and picked my way tentatively into the water, until I could lower myself to swim. The water struck bitterly cold despite the sunshine. It lapped repeatedly against my chest, like the anxious movement of a cow's tail trying to brush a pest from her back. I felt suddenly mistrustful, vulnerable, alone in an alien element, a great fluidity that stretched indefinitely before me, in which I must struggle to be supported and moved forward. I looked up, and Rawiri was already far away, a distant black head dipping in and out of the glistening water with a seemingly effortless joy. He trod water for a moment, and shouted to me to catch up with him. But I sat there shivering, unable to move.

Later we lit a fire, and barbecued sausages and bacon and tomatoes, and made billy tea, and ate the blackberries. When the light faded, we went into the wooden house and lit candles; it always pleased and amazed me what comfort could come from sparse resources. We played cards by candlelight, drank the bottle of wine we had brought with us; and then sat in silence, staring at the floor in the flickering light, distant intermittent music from the transistor in the background. A huhu-beetle had found its way in through the open window, drawn by the candles, and was whirring and thudding helplessly about somewhere in the half-light.

Getting to know Rawiri had been the most important revelation of my life. We were both outsiders, outcasts almost. For a start, we were both gay, with all the sharp vision of a lonely pauper staring through a rich man's window that can bring. And then, I had left my country and my culture in disillusion: he had been taken from his people and what might have been his culture, to be brought up almost a stranger in his own land, at home in neither camp. I think neither of us had realised these things with any intensity until we knew one another. With one another we became the first community to which we had ever felt we belonged.

And yet there remained certain barriers in our community, which I respected, which I could never have tried to knock down; but which I did not understand. To me it seemed it should all have been so simple. I suppose I had grown up thinking, like many people, that the only way in from the outside was marriage, and of course, I know I have saved myself and others much deprivation because that door was closed to me. But between you and me what I dreamed of was perhaps little less than marriage. A reactionary dream? I might know that, but the dream would not leave me, it followed me like a stray dog begging to be adopted.

The silence between us had become long. As you and I often did at such times, we began to talk about life after the revolution. To discuss the world as a distant abstraction can often give one a reassurance the material world is rarely able to.

'Peter. Do you really look forward to the revolution?' said Rawiri quietly into the candlelight, his huge Maori eyes still and innocent, like fish in a clear creek.

'The revolution, yes,' I said, clutching my knees, and resting my head on them for a moment before I went on. 'But not the times leading up to it, not the deprivation seeping through like a slow corrosion, not the frustrated violence, not the lagging growth of knowledge. So many false starts, so many disappointments. The realisation that so much must be abandoned, and so much waits to be built. And yet, as it is when one is in pain, how intensely alive one must feel then.'

'Some of our friends wouldn't like to hear you talk so pessimistically, eh?' said Rawiri, his face flaring up with a bright smile, the darkness of his eyes swamped by the whiteness of his teeth. 'That's the time that gives purpose to our lives, brother.'

'Yes, yes, I know,' I said, and found myself smiling back.

Because what you said made me happy. And we smiled with one another for a while. I said 'Anyway, we can't go back, and we can't just jump forward.' And my happiness seemed to go away for a moment, as if it had passed behind a cloud.

'I'll try to do the best I can,' said Rawiri quietly, furrowing his brow. 'And then, in a sane world, we'll all look after one another, even when life is hard. And that's not a dream, eh?'

The cloud passed away again. 'No,' I said, 'it's not a dream: it's a result.'

Rawiri yawned, and rubbed his eyes carelessly with the hands that were so careful to others. 'I'm tired now. Time for bed.'

I waited for you to ask me to sleep with you, and you did.

'We'll sleep together, eh?' Rawiri said, a soft little brush of sound.

When we lay in one another's arms, it seemed as if the touch of our moving hands was so gentle that we almost did not touch at all, because we were both so fragile. Beneath your exploring fingers I felt myself become a land moulded by its history, down my sides you followed river-beds worn by consolation, by my eyes you sheltered at lakes in rifts opened by disappointment, along my thighs you climbed mountains raised by expectation. Uncertain, I wandered in awe among the warm sunlit stretches and the moist shades of your body.

Though it seemed as if it was not true, I made myself say to him, 'Why do we sleep together so rarely? And why does it stop here? I don't understand.'

'Peter. I know it's not all you want,' Rawiri said, resignedly, softly, laying the inadequate words over me as he might have lain his jacket over my injured body in a desolate place. Even in the darkness I could see his eyes glowing across the pillow. 'But I'm haunted by dreams — you must have noticed really, eh? — fantasies about powerful men — I mean, the usual white images of powerful, dominating men. I keep trying to shake them off, but it's as if they're tied to me; as if they were purposefully tied to me when I was a child. Of course, I *know* those images are shit, I know them for what they are. They're just a key part of the structure of our oppression. Of our system even. I want to destroy them as much as you do. But that only makes the fantasies more unreal: it doesn't take them away. Yeah, I used to think, like you do, "one day, Pete and I, we'll be together." Yeah. And yet I can't get rid of what I was told to grow up wanting, even if I don't really want it and now never will.'

He stopped. For a moment I stared at the ceiling, listening to the sound of his breathing, aware of nothing more than warmth and moisture where his hand lay on my shoulder, mine on his.

'I try to do the best I can, brother,' he said tenderly.

I said your name in a whisper, 'Rawiri'. The first stressed syllable, bright, vigorous, opening out; the others falling away in a murmur. 'Rawiri,' I said to him, 'it's alright, it's alright, it's alright.' I wanted to pour the words over him as if they were warm water washing his tired and bleeding feet on a long journey. He nestled his head against my shoulder, I could feel the kindly warmth of his breath coming and going against my skin, as his shoulders rose and then fell again. I ran my hand among the black waves of his hair, stroking, reassuring.

You and I, we bathed one another in tenderness: but we are part of a time made of rocks that do not just wear away.

He said quietly, 'When we live in a meagre world, we have to share what we can, eh? We shouldn't really want things that belong to an emotional plenty that doesn't yet exist.'

After a while I realised he had fallen asleep. I was alone with my thoughts. Perhaps the best we can hope for in our private lives is a kind of righteous yearning.

I was exhausted, but I could not sleep. For a long time I lay awake in the warm summer night, struggling with my longings, listening to the huhu somewhere in the darkness, starting up, whirring for a moment, then crashing into the wall, trying ceaselessly to escape the place into which it had been attracted.

The next morning was heavy and overcast. The lake was lit by a light like that of a sepia photograph. We got up late, put together some breakfast, made jokes with one another for a bit, read for a while. We had to leave the next day. In the late afternoon we decided to take the boat and go across the lake to the main road so that we could have a meal in the motel. It rained heavily while we were there, and we waited for it to stop. When we finally came to leave, it was already getting dark. A strange yellowish darkness. The bush-covered hills had become a black reclining figure.

We were out in the middle of the lake when the engine cut out. I tried to hold the boat in a straight line, while Rawiri stood trying unsuccessfully to restart the engine. Darkness stole down over the lake, and a quiet that one could almost feel. I put my hand in the lapping water, and it felt warm and soft, almost inviting. A morepork called, far away in the distance. And nothing moved. Everything was dead still. Expectant.

'It's wonderful,' said Rawiri softly, poised holding the end of the rewound starter-rope in his hand.

It was a frightening beautiful moment. I felt intensely alive.

ME AND MR MANDEL

by Eric Presland

Let's get one thing clear. I don't take no lip from nobody. Nobody puts one over on me, I can tell you. So when they told me, I nearly hit the roof. I went right up the bloody wall, and that's a fact. I mean, fifteen pounds! For the love of God, where can you get a coffin for fifteen pounds these days? And that's not counting the rabbi's fees, never mind a stone or some flowers. How can you have a decent funeral without flowers?

I went straight down the dole office, and I told them. I gave it to them straight. Fifty years he'd worked. Twelve hours a day, six days a week. Worked his fingers to the bone, he did. But did it make any difference? Did it, be buggered — excuse my French, miss. It's always the same old story. Those people got hearts of stone. Look what happened with the pension. Seventy he was before he got that. And all because he wanted to keep doing a bit of work! Is it a sin to want to work? Is it a crime? I ask you.

Do you know what they told me down the dole office? 'He hasn't paid his contributions.' He'd come into the scheme too late, they said. Half the Death Grant and that was that. Contributions! He'd paid his taxes. He'd earned it. Why, his whole life was a contribution.

It was a young fellow down the dole. Couldn't have been more than — oh, twenty at most. He had long hair down on his shoulders, and an earring through his ear — Jesus, like a bloody woman, he was. And there he is, this little nancy boy, standing there calm as you like, telling me Mr Mandel's only going to get fifteen pounds! Well, I lost me temper. I got a terrible temper sometimes. My wife'd tell you — God rest her soul — sometimes I just blow me top. And the little ponce is standing there giving me all this rubbish, and me thinking of Mr Mandel at his sewing machine these fifty years, and — well, I'd had a few pints at lunchtime — but I didn't mean to break the window, miss, honest.

It was an accident. It was only a little window, couldn't have been worth more than a few bob. It was the drink talking, miss. What did he want to call the police like that for? I'm old enough to be his grandfather. I didn't mean any harm, miss. I just wanted to see him done right by.

You see, he lived for his work, did Mr Mandel. Even after he'd retired he wouldn't give it up. We'd be sitting in our little parlour of an evening, I'd do me pools or have a read of the paper, but he'd always be patching up some trousers or running up a blouse from some odds and ends he'd picked up at a jumble sale. He used to haunt those jumble sales. Little scraps he used to pick up, said they'd come in handy some time. And he was right. He liked to keep himself busy. And if it was for children, there was nothing he wouldn't do. They was always in and out the house for a bit of bread and jam. He was a gentleman, you see. A real gentleman. Educated too — went to a proper Jewish school. Not like me. I left school at twelve — well, you had to in those days.

They asked me down the dole office what Mr Mandel was to me. They said it was 'all in the hands of the social services'. But I don't want him shovelled into the ground by the council, some pauper's grave, without so much as a by-your-leave.

It's not as if I can do anything myself. I had a few bob put by — well he put it by for me really — but since he got took ill and went up the hospital, the house got sort of quiet. The kids stopped coming round. I took to going up the pub a bit. And the drink's always been the temptation with me. So now it's all gone. The money's gone, the kids gone, he's gone. There's nothing left . . .

I'm sorry, miss. I didn't mean to do that. You must think I'm soft, or something.

Oh, thank you miss. I'd love one. Two sugars, please.

You see, it's not as if he had anybody else. The family's all dead. Not that he ever had much time for them. And he never got married or anything like that. Actually, if the truth be told, I think he was a bit frightened by women. He wasn't the marrying kind, if you know what I mean. So there's only me. And I want to see him done right by.

Cos fifteen years is a long time. Course, when you get to my age it goes a lot faster, but fifteen years is still fifteen years. I got to pay him back for his kindness.

Cos I was in a terrible state when I met him. Me wife had just died. I took to the drink then too. Never washed. Rags on my back. Terrible. And he changed all that.

I remember, I was standing in the Post Office. I'd just collected me pension. It was about a month after my wife died, and I'd never been to collect on my own before. I couldn't put her out of me mind. And there, between the queues, I just broke down. Howled like a babby. I kept remembering. One night we'd gone to bed, same as usual, and when I woke up in the morning, there she was, lying beside me, cold. She'd just gone in the night, never even made a noise or anything. Never even woke me up. Mind you, I've always been a heavy sleeper. Perhaps she tried . . . And there in the Post Office, I thought how cold she'd been, and I couldn't stop myself.

He came over and put his hand on my shoulder, took me to the caff next door. You know what they say about Jewish mothers? Well, he was just like that. Sat opposite saying 'Eat, eat' , and me sitting there staring at a plate of beans. He was right, of course. I hadn't touched a thing for days — well, you don't bother when you're on your own, do you?

He took me to his house, and made me have a wash and a bit of a lie-down till I felt a bit better. And I told him about my wife and things. And how the council wanted to move me to a single flat with a load of old people. Jesus, think of that! Load of old biddies fussing around. I'd go up the wall. Well, we talked things over, and there he was with his spare room he didn't need, and wondering how he was going to make ends meet now he'd been 'put out to grass' — that's what he called it. And to cut a long story short, he let me move in. Into his own home. 'Paying guest,' he said.

So we settled into our little ways. I helped him with the dole office when he had troubles — you see, he'd worked all his life, he'd never had to bother with them before. It came as a bit of a shock to have to go down there. He didn't like making a fuss. Didn't want charity. 'Charity be blowed, Mr Mandel,' I said. 'It's your bloody right. You've earned it.' And I made those buggers sit up and take notice, I can tell you. I could help round the house too, as I was in the building trade. He'd let that place go something terrible. Half the floorboards were rotten. I doubt if he'd even noticed. Never had time, what with all the tailoring. And he took care of all the money and the shopping. I paid all my pension to him, he let me have a few bob for fags. I've never had a head for figures, but he had it all worked out. I never realised how much he'd saved for me, till he told me when he was took sick at last. And on a Friday or Saturday we'd go out down the pub or to the pictures together.

So we got along. It was — it was a real home. Sometimes I'd miss my wife, to be sure, but he understood that, even though he hadn't been married himself. Marvellous sympathy that man had. It was a great comfort.

Do you understand what I'm saying, miss? I loved that man. Loved him. Don't get me wrong, there wasn't anything funny about it, I'm not like that, bent or anything. But it was comfortable. It was always comfortable. Like, I'd get a bit of bronchitis on my chest in the damp months, and he'd always be there with a bit of whisky and hot lemon, or a drop of Vick to rub on my chest. Such cool gentle hands he had. Touch like velvet.

Being ill on your own's a terrible thing. I was took bad after he went up the hospital. Most miserable time of my life. Clock ticking on the landing, not a sound in the house. Couldn't hardly move. Terrible.

First day I was back on my feet, I went straight up to the hospital to see him — cos I used to go and see him every day. Oh yes. And, d'you know, when I got there he was so worried. Not for himself, but for me. 'Are you all right, Michael? Should you be out so soon? Are you looking after yourself?' He was worried about me. And him lying there dying.

I hated going up that place. Hated it. It was converted from an old workhouse. And I remember when it was a workhouse. Little windows high up on the walls. Bars over them. All them smells. I think I took it worse than he did. He was very good about it. Very patient. 'Won't be long now, Michael,' he used to say. But the marvellous thing was, he never lost his interest. Always wanted to know what was going on. The nurses loved him.

Towards the end I couldn't face going up there without a drink or two. I used to smuggle in a drop of brandy for the two of us, till the Sister caught me. After that I went down the pub first. One day I had a bit more than usual. I hadn't been eating or sleeping either, what with the worry. When I got to the ward, he was going. They said he was asleep and couldn't see me, but I could tell from their eyes he hadn't long. 'Let me in,' I begged. I pleaded with them, the tears streaming down me face like a girl. 'You've got to let me in. He's in there bloody dying.' Didn't make a blind bit of difference. Not next of kin, they said. Not a relative, they said. After fifteen years.

A couple of porters took me out. But I wasn't going to give in so easy. I waited till the porters had gone, and I nipped round the side of the building. Sure enough, there was a toilet window there — you know the sort; a big window underneath and a little window on the top. There weren't any bars on the big window and the little window was open.

I went over to the kitchens, and there was a couple of milk crates outside, so I dragged one of them over — me bad leg was killing me — and got up on top of it. I reached in through the little window, but I couldn't get the catch on the big window, so I took my stick and smashed it. I wasn't going to let him go, just like that.

They called the police then too. Said I was disturbing the other patients. Oh, but they knew all right. Cos, as they was taking me down the nick I heard them talking in the front of the car. 'What's the trouble' says the driver. 'Nothing,' says the copper, 'some old poof kicked the bucket, this is his boyfriend.' 'What, him?' says the driver. 'Ought to be past it at his age, dirty old bugger.' I could have killed him. I would have killed him, but I hadn't the strength left. I was too exhausted even to cry.

Lucky the magistrate was kind. Otherwise I'd never have got out in time to find out. Cos they can't keep him in the — down there for ever, even with the strike on. And they wouldn't even tell me where he was going to. Do you think you can do anything, miss? Mrs Khan next door told me you help people up here with the social security and the damp and things. It's not much to ask, is it? A decent burial with a few flowers and a bit of music. He'd have liked that — very fond of music he was. Brass bands was his favourite.

If you could try. Thursday? I'll be in. Thank you. I'm sorry to take up your time. I wouldn't have bothered you over a little thing like this, but there's nowhere else to go, see?

Oh, no, thank you very much. I don't want no social workers sniffing around. Asking questions, moving the furniture. I can stand on my own feet. Don't you worry about me. I can manage. But I do miss him. He was a wonderful man.

Well, you been a great help, miss. I'll see myself out — if you could just pass me stick? Thank you. I'll see you on Thursday, then.

And thanks for the tea.

CODA

by DuMont Howard

Her face. The long, rather aquiline nose, the full lips, the startling green eyes (her best feature), the drifts of dark wavy hair and — yes, there was no doubt about it — two anxious lines stretching up the middle of her forehead from her nose.

She sighed and picked up the foundation base and put it down again. Those lines had made themselves known for the first time today, when Rodney Albert had shown her the proofs from last week's session for the cover of the new album. And there they had been. Frighteningly evident, particularly in one picture where she was laughing, her face rumpled and squeezed. 'Oh, dear. I look *dreadful*,' she had laughed, clutching Rodney's arm. But all the same she had felt cross and dismayed.

She leaned closer to the mirror of her dressing-table, peering more closely to determine the extent of the damage. They were not so evident here, for the dressing-room mirror was lit for the stage, but they were definitely there and certain to further define themselves in the future. 'Well, it doesn't matter,' she said aloud, with an abrupt defiant shrug, and then let her mind rest for a moment on the prospect of plastic surgery. She had been robbed, she wanted to cry out; at thirty-two she was too young to have these wrinkles. At dinner with Rodney, after he had shown her the photos, she had cast furtive glances at the other women in the restaurant, checking on the state of their foreheads and calculating their ages relative to hers. It was all the fault of this heavy stage make-up, she concluded with irritation, looking down at the bottles and tubes and boxes spread before her. They had ruined her skin.

Damn. This was just silly. 'A face is nothing until it gets broken in,' was what her mother would say. But *she* didn't have to go on stage every night. Thank God this was closing night. Then six weeks of rest. And how she needed it! She picked up the

foundation and began sponging it on decisively. It was something
of a comfort, even the familiar, damp musty smell of the pad. And
next week at this time she would be married, she reminded herself,
studying her image in the mirror. Mrs Gerald Freeman.

She had nothing to complain about. By all accounts her
existence had taken a decided turn for the better. Even she
wouldn't have dared envision this pleasing outcome when, four
years ago, determined that if she had to re-type one more business
letter life wasn't worth living, she had quit her secretarial job to
take a fling at a singing career. 'You're wasting your time,' her
mother had fumed, 'you're no singer.' 'You're crazy,' Maxine, her
old girlfriend from next door, had affirmed with a dispassionate
shrug. And there were many moments, when she was trouping
from singer-showcase to open-mike nights and bouncing in and
out of temp work to keep herself going, that she knew they were
right. But that sink-or-swim struggle had had its own momentum.
Keep going was the thought she kept pulsing insistently through
her brain, when audiences seemed indifferent, when she got
panned, when the first recording contract fell through. And now,
how many times in the last two years, in front of the endless
succession of dressing-room mirrors or waiting in the wings
hearing the audience applauding *her* overture, composed of *her*
hits, had she stopped short and crowed to herself *I did it, I showed
them, I pulled it off. The gangly, never-singled-out girl from Lenox
Avenue is a big success.* Her first album, one of the countless
albums by new and soon-forgotten girl singers, had been an
unexpected hit. Even the executives at RCA had been surprised,
though they began cheerfully pumping what seemed like enor-
mous sums into promotion. And after all those years, those
unending days of struggle, she had, it seemed, become a star
overnight. The money flowed, she was heard on the radio, she was
booked on the big television shows, songwriters sent her songs,
posters announcing her concerts were to be found on walls and she
hadn't had to paste them there herself.

And then the first blush of wonder had worn off. Not just for
her, but seemingly for everyone. With several hit albums behind
her, a Grammy nomination this year and talk of her own television
special, her career was at a fever pitch, but everyone seemed to feel
the pitch should be raised an extra notch. She must move ahead or
she would fall back. The sales on her last album hadn't fulfilled
rising expectations. What about a disco album? urged Columbia.
What about a Broadway show? Her agent had pushed the idea of a
movie and she had been more than susceptible to the visions he

conjured of movie stardom. They settled on a 'surefire' script, signed a contract and last spring she had found herself among strangers in a Los Angeles studio in the midst of a doomed film production, rushing out, on her breaks, to slip pocketfuls of dimes into the pay phone in the hall, in an effort to get advice from her nowhere-to-be-found agent.

But as unsettling as these decisions were and as much as she hated the pressure, she knew that she did have to move ahead or she would fall back. The threat of falling back took form in the prospect of her face becoming one of those that haunt game shows and uneventful guest spots on television series. It was no comfort to realise that she had come such a long way when she still had so far to go. That she had been so embarrassingly awful when she started out only seemed to underline the present indecision. How horrified she had been several weeks ago, when she had caught a re-run of one of her first talk-show appearances. How gauche she had seemed. All intensity and no technique. She had suffered a million agonies watching her former self; her pitch had been faulty, she moved awkwardly, and why had she ever worn her hair that way? She winced now at the thought of it, as she pencilled in her eyebrows. Yet how pleased she had been at the time. What was she like now? She glared interrogatingly at the image in the mirror. What was the right direction to take? She had become a success with her stylised renditions of old standards and middle-of-the-road versions of old AM radio hits. But the market for this material was too limited, the RCA people kept insisting. It was exhausting. Recently she had caught herself wondering what she was in it for. Why had she decided to become a singer? What dreams had filled the hours she had spent listening to worn-out Billie Holiday and Judy Garland on her old portable? Was it the aura of glamour, adulation and money that had so captured her sixteen-year-old imagination? Certainly she was fascinated with the accoutrements of her present life: the gleaming limos, the pastel-pink music folder with her name embossed on it, the irridescent bouquets, the sputter of camera shutters. Or was it the music itself that had drawn her to gamble on a singing career? Please God let it be the music. She felt that she had learned that the other things, while satisfying, had their limitations. Large sums of money were within her grasp if she cared to use her name to hawk Polaroid cameras or sing the praises of Coke. Residuals! her agent had crowed, but to his bitter incomprehension she turned down all the offers. That had been difficult enough, but the growing insistence by everyone around her that she become a disco or rock singer was truly bewildering. There were millions of such performers around. She had made her success as a chanteuse, but for some reason that was no longer good enough. Didn't they understand? She hadn't spent all those afternoons drowning herself in each of Billie Holiday's inflections and emotional nuances for nothing. She wanted to be an artist, capital A, and yet she had realised too late that she hadn't a strong enough concept of exactly what kind of artist she was going to be.

Well, she would be married soon, she reassured herself, once again applying that soothing balm. Her worried gaze spotted an area she had missed with the pad. There was only one problem with the marriage. Gerald was gay. She sighed and laid down the pad. Here was one blemish which Max Factor pancake couldn't cover. Well, of course she didn't know *for sure* that he was gay, she reminded herself. What's more, if he was, she was positive he himself didn't have an inkling. It was very careless of him, to say the least. If she had been a lesbian, she was certain she wouldn't have required anyone to tell *her*. And she was definitely no expert on homosexuality.

She would never have even suspected Gerald was gay if it hadn't been for Tony, the man who cut her hair. Last Thursday Gerald had walked her over to the salon and sat with her for a few moments while she waited for Tony to become free. After Gerald left for an appointment she thumbed through a gossip magazine, reading with fascination a fatuous article about her upcoming marriage.

'Handsome man,' murmured Tony when she had finally gotten into the chair. He surveyed her hair, then caught her glance in the mirror and smiled. 'Is he attached?'

'Not yet,' she had responded happily.

'Then you'll have to introduce us,' said Tony, picking up the scissors.

'Yes,' she had answered, or maybe 'certainly' in a vague pleasant way. She was thinking of other things. She was doing the Carson show that night and troubling over the scarlet dress she had chosen to wear — too loud? Maybe she should have stuck with the black one with the beaded neck. Television shots were still infrequent and it wouldn't do not to put her best foot forward.

Only later, sitting off-camera in the green room waiting to go on, numbly watching the ongoing show on the monitor, had the conversation re-surfaced and made her aware of its true nature: *Tony hadn't realised that the man with her was Gerald, the man she was going to marry. Tony had had his eye on Gerald. Tony thought*

Gerald was gay.

She picked up a broad stumpy brush and starting applying blush to her cheekbones. Since the night she had walked dazed through her *Tonight Show* appearance, she had tried to dismiss the interchange with Tony, but it stuck stubbornly, replaying itself over and over again in the back of her head. To her dismay she found herself examining Gerald for tell-tale signs. She began running all the details of their joint existence through her brain, peering at them again from this new angle. He had been a virgin when they first slept together (or so he claimed and his nervousness had seemed to confirm it). This had charmed her at the time, now she couldn't help wondering if it was — she cringed at the word — normal for a twenty-six-year-old man to be a virgin. She noticed that when gay men were around he fell noticeably silent and, several times, had made rather implausible excuses to get away. Doubt began to cast its malignancy everywhere; she caught herself gauging the affection and sincerity in each kiss and embrace. The last week, with Gerald away on a business trip, had been a relief; there had been no new evidence to weigh, no new questions to ask. She had done her best to push the whole matter aside.

Oh dear. Marriage to Gerald had promised to solidify the private sector of her life and hopefully diminish the threatening indecision which plagued the public sector, her career. How many times had she enticed herself with the comforting 'Well, if it becomes too much, I'll just give it all up. I'll abandon the nomadic existence — the concerts, the guest shots, the running around — and settle down with Gerald'. But she knew that this fantasy, even at its most comforting, was only a delusion. Certainly Gerald's income would support them both, but she could never leave performing behind. *Could she?* The gnawing underlying fear was that it was this public person, the woman on the stage, the beloved chanteuse, that was her ace, her drawing card, and without her she would once again be the girl who had no dates, who brownbagged her lunch with the girls from the secretarial pool, who whiled away Friday and Saturday evening watching television with her mother. Her advisors were right; if she did not move ahead, she would slip back.

But now she could no longer entertain notions of retiring to marital bliss even as fantasy. Gerald could not save her from the vagaries of her career. She stared at her blank expression in the mirror. She could not see herself sitting down with Gerald and telling him they must not marry because he was queer. No, the situation was impossible. She could not even flee. The marriage, thanks to the shameless ingenuity of her agent, was already too public an affair; newspapers, television and radio would chart any escape. She checked her watch; seven o'clock — she still had a little time before backstage would be thronged with people vying for her attention. But she went over to the door and locked it anyway.

It isn't fair, she wailed silently, once again depositing herself in front of the mirror. She was not equipped for this situation. She still didn't know enough about homosexuality. In high school there had been several effeminate boys who had been called 'fairy' and 'pansy.' And later, of course, on the periphery of her awareness there were homosexuals marching and protesting, newspaper articles, bits on the evening news, books. But none of it ever quite managed to intrude on the main line of her vision.

Until she began singing regularly. One night, during one of her early engagements, she had been happily conversing with several fans who stayed after the show to see her, when she realised that two of the men had, quite casually, slipped their arms around each other's waist. And she knew instantly, in a crashing revelation, that the fans — all men — who had come to see her were gay. The discovery thoroughly unnerved her. During her sets the next night she scanned the audiences, finding only a few women and a dis-proportionate number of men. It upset her to think that she had been in the midst of this without sensing it.

Through that initial period of discomfort and displacement she had bluffed her way, all the while registering from the corner of her eye each brush of hands, each pat on the behind. God, what a naive, priggish fool she had been. Now she talked easily with her gay fans, made jokes, asked about personal relationships, teased them. She had been horrified when her mother had come to see her last fall, pulled her aside after the show and hissed with conspira-torial urgency 'The audience — all fagellas!'

'So what,' she had snapped back coldly, turning away and hoping no one had overheard the exchange.

But if she was no longer uncomfortable, she was still an outsider. Absurd that reporters should question her about her 'gay appeal', when all she knew was that these nice young men brought her flowers, thought her witty, were devoted to her singing, collected her records, and, unlike all the boys she had known, made her feel attractive and special. Now she had been dealt a cruel trick; she had unwittingly become engaged to one of these nice young men.

But the point. What was the point of all this? Too many things had become intertwined and now churned about her head in a hopeless tangle: Gerald, her career, sex, growing old, feeling insecure. The immediate point, she ventured cautiously, seemed to be that she could not, no matter what, marry Gerald. The rest could wait. But how was she to cancel a marriage that was a mere four days away? There was no one she could enlist to advise her, least of all her mother or Maxine. And not her agent. Milton would feel obliged to point out that she had her career to think of. Gerald was a propitious match: wealth, family background and fair-haired good looks. But though she had certainly been aware of these things (what girl from Lenox Avenue wouldn't be?), she had not chosen him for these reasons. That the press, her agent and her fans so openly revelled in the Cinderella-poor-girl-from-Bronx-marries-WASP-prince aspect of the marriage shocked her. She was quite sure that her affection for Gerald was free of such considerations. After all, she'd had that proposition from that gleaming six-feet-four Texas businessman, the owner of a fast-food chain, who had clasped her tiny white hand in his huge bronzed paw with the opal ring on the pinky and asked her if she'd marry him or be his mistress, and she had turned him down without a thought for his chiselled tawny features, sea-blue eyes or fast-food millions.

No. She liked Gerald and maybe even loved him. His stillness, his concentration, his sudden, shy flashing grins. He had first appeared on her opening night at Carnegie Hall among the swarm that buzzed about her dressing-room after the show, the show that, as one endearing critic had put it, 'firmly established her as the finest new singer of the last ten years'. There, in her bower bursting with flowers, her well-wishers were courting her and she was, as her mother had drily remarked, 'putting on the dog', playing the glamorous, gracious, luminous lady, captivating them, animatedly dispensing quips and cracks and wanton wiles, nods and becks and wreathed smiles; in short, behaving in a fashion which in saner moments she knew to be perfectly disgusting. Flinging herself about the room, the wings of her new flowered silk kimono fluttering as she planted precious kisses or bestowed fleeting hugs, beacon-like she searched out every untapped source of gushing admiration. And so she had spotted Gerald, standing in the corner, a small neat man in a dark blue business suit, watching her, watching the others, with an armoured smile.

She eyed him briefly with mistrust; a bored interloper in her squadron of sycophants. She had encountered this type before: brought to the show (which he hadn't enjoyed) and now backstage by a more gregarious friend, a fan. Still, she speculated, checking him out from the corner of her eye, he seemed to be alone. Well, he'd go soon.

A few minutes later, making her rounds of the dressing-room, she turned from the glowing report of one admirer, prepared to look for the next, and found herself staring face to face with him.

'Hello,' she blurted out awkwardly, startled out of her graciousness.

'Hello.' He grinned. 'I wanted to tell you that I liked your show.' She was wondering why this comparatively mild remark should seem so flattering, when he produced a small bouquet of violets and handed them to her.

The face in the mirror was dreamy. It would not be easy to give up Gerald. It would be a long time before she found someone she liked as well, who did not find her career threatening, but took innocent pleasure in it (Gerald was excited every time he found her name in a magazine, newspaper or television listing), who was so amiable, content and gentle.

It just wasn't fair, she thought again rebelliously, gazing sympathetically at the figure that watched her mournfully from the mirror. She could not carry this out alone; she would have to talk to Gerald. Yes, she firmly said aloud. She *had* to talk to him; he was, after all, the groom. Well, that at least was a definite relief. What couldn't be helped, couldn't be helped. She uncapped the lipstick and pouted her lips, painting them with Festival, the colour the woman at Elizabeth Arden had insisted would be ideal for her. She would talk to him soon. She would talk to him tonight when he got back from his business trip. No, she would not worry about how to broach the subject until the time came. She smacked her lips and noted with satisfaction that she had applied the lipstick evenly and symmetrically.

A knock at the door and jiggling of the knob. 'Darling?'

She caught her startled alarm in the glass. She searched her face for tell-tale smears of guilt. She had been caught in the middle of secret traitorous thoughts; surely she had left evidence somewhere. 'Gerald?' she called back tentatively, finally springing up from the dressing-table to unlock the door.

'I thought you weren't getting back until later,' she cried, flinging herself into his arms.

'But here I am,' he said cheerfully.

'Yes.' She flopped back into her chair. He dragged over the armchair and sat down.

'You're kind of early yourself; I didn't think I had a chance of finding you here. Did you have dinner yet?'

'Oh? Yes. I had dinner with Rodney.' She stared down at the clutter on her dressing-table, trying to concentrate.

'Miss me?'

'Of course,' she rallied, smiling bravely she thought. And then she realised he looked exhausted. 'How was it?'

He leaned back in the chair and closed his eyes. 'Oh, it was boring. How about you?'

'Busy mostly. I need the break.' To demonstrate, she picked up the eyeshadow and busily applied it, still eyeing him from the mirror. He nodded, his eyes still closed. How worn out he looked. She took up the eyeliner. Perhaps she should not talk to him tonight.

'Actually, I came back early to talk to you,' he let out in a rush.

She had smudged the eyeliner.

'I don't know how to begin.'

She waited, frozen there, watching her blinking eye further blotch the eyeliner, her fingers still clenching the inactive brush. What, she interrogated herself furiously, did he want to talk about? Finally he opened his eyes. Their gazes met in their reflections; what miserable people they seemed. She grabbed for a tissue to mend the eyeliner.

'Well, begin at the beginning,' she mumbled with utterly false cheer, all the while shielding her face with the tissue. 'This is it,' cried the tension in her stomach, as she kept the white fluff dabbing vigorously at her make-up. 'Something about your trip?' she suggested helpfully.

'Well, yes and no.' She waited. 'I don't know how to begin,' he repeated.

She had never seen him so distraught. It tore her apart to see him this unhappy; the situation was far more desperate and alarming than she had imagined.

'Are you gay?' she heard herself whisper.

Gerald's head jerked up and they stared at each other, shocked by her question. The colour drained from his face; she couldn't bear to look at him. Turning back to the mirror she found that she too was quite pale. Behind her reflection she saw Gerald shift in his chair, his gaze returning to the floor. How had she dared voice the question? And what if she were wrong?

Just as the tone of her silent interrogation seemed to become unbearably shrill, he broke the silence. 'Yes,' he said softly, 'I think I am.' After a brief pause he continued in an undertone. On the flight to L.A. he had sat next to a very friendly man, an architect. They'd had a nice chat on the flight and he told Gerald to call if he had some free time. And, unexpectedly, Tuesday night there had been a cancelled meeting, a spare evening. Gerald had been in the neighbourhood. He phoned and was invited to stop by for a drink. The man had a lovely house overlooking the beach and was very pleased to see him. They listened to some music and Gerald was shown the plans for the architect's latest project. They'd had a few martinis and were sitting side by side on the couch when the man kissed him on the neck.

As the story progressed Gerald's tone lightened and expanded. She listened dully, helplessly staring at the litter of her cosmetics as the tale made its inexorable progress. It was as if she knew the story already; there were no surprises. Gerald had resisted after a time, politely, had finally even gotten somewhat indignant and stalked out, cheeks burning, stomach knotted, mind in turmoil. But after blindly fleeing several blocks in the opposite direction of his car, he had realised that he'd left his overcoat behind and had no choice but to go back.

Gerald stopped and looked at the floor. The spiralling apologetic, pleading, explanatory tone of his narrative hung in the air. She yearned for something, anything, to happen — a violent, disruptive, arbitrary incident which would blissfully hurl them from the room, detach them from the confines of their melodrama, an explosion or sudden fire which would shatter the mirror and singe the armchair. Instead, she picked up the eyeliner again, drew a delicate perfect oval around her left eye and proceeded to do an only slightly less perfect job on the right one. Then, without turning, she reached out her hand and patted his knee. She wanted to say something reassuring, but found it impossible to formulate anything appropriate. Certainly this was a new role for her and she wondered if other people would have responded differently: cried or screamed or been highly insulted or icily cold. She felt only numb; there was no longer anything left to settle or dispute, only the whole exacting business of everyday life to face, their individual walking papers, their own separate lots to hoe. She had a concert to do, a career to navigate, the hole Gerald had left to patch. His concerns lay in exploring his gayness, discovering himself. She couldn't help feeling he had gotten the best of the deal. It wasn't fair, but there it was.

Someone tapped at the door. She hoped she had remembered to re-lock it.

'Yes?' she said finally, tentatively, her voice sounding dry and brittle.

'Anybody seen my client?' queried Milton through the door.

'I think she retired and moved to Kansas. Come back in ten minutes.'

'Everything okay? You've only got half an hour till curtain.'

'Yes, everything's peachy. Go away.' And he did; she heard him move hesitantly down the hall and knew he was wondering if he should be worrying about her. She checked her watch; he was right. What had happened to the time? she thought irritably, surveying her make-up for what remained to be done, fussing with her false eyelashes. Milton's interruption had brought a barrage of anxiety with it, a sea of inquiring faces — gossip columnists, reporters, fans — all of them wanting to know *why?* And she would not moan or cry or sulk. And she most certainly wouldn't say that she and Gerald had decided he would be better off with another man. No, she would smile discreetly and purr, over and over again until it seemed true, a statement that she and Milton would hammer out. She would field questions in a few interviews, trade some smart quips with Johnny Carson about being single again and eventually it would be over. People would stop asking and interest would soon — alarmingly quickly, really — move to some other issue. But when she had finished answering everyone else's questions, there would still be her own, tirelessly waiting in ambush for her. And then, she knew, the hurt would start. She must ask Milton to arrange some work for the next two weeks; she couldn't bear the thought of two weeks of inactivity in which to confront her thoughts.

Gerald's hands on her shoulders interrupted her reverie. 'I better let you get ready.' She had almost forgotten he was there. 'I'm sorry. It was wrong of me to bother you before the show.'

She turned and looked up at him and shook her head, trying for a grin. He leaned down and kissed her. A sweet, gentle kiss, one that already registered the change in their relationship. 'I'll be back after the show,' he murmured. And he left.

She checked for the millionth time, as she did tonight and every night, night after night, for stray marks, smudges and smears, but everything seemed in place. There was nothing to do now but wait for her cue.

ONE OF THE RISKS

by David Rees

Nicky sat in the station refreshment-room, finishing his cup of tea. The man on the other side of the table was young, not much older than himself, but strong, the games-playing type. He was blond, too, sunburnt and good-looking; he sat casually at ease, one foot kicked out, hands resting on the chair between his legs, almost arrogant in appearance.

'Have another cup?' the man asked.

'Thank you,' said Nicky, excited by the invitation. 'It's very kind of you.'

When he returned with the teas, the man sat next to Nicky on the long wall-seat. Their arms and legs touched. Nicky looked at him out of the corner of his eye. Outside was the hullabaloo of people running for trains and the thundering shudder of an express engine testing out its strength.

'Like to come back with me?' the man said in a voice just above a whisper. 'I don't live far away. It's quite safe, self-contained flat. You can stay the night if you want to.'

Nicky looked at him a long moment without speaking. 'Yes,' he said at last, his heart beating a little faster. 'I can't stop long, but I'll come.'

'I've got a car here, parked just round the back.'

'So have I — '

'Oh have you? We'll go in yours then; there's room only for one parking. The name's Tom, by the way. What's yours?'

'Nicky.'

'Nice to meet you, Nicky. Not working today?'

'I've finished. I'm on teaching practice; I'm a student.'

'Oh, boys' school? What are they like, eh? Any good?' Nicky laughed, embarrassed. 'Come on, aren't there any you fancy? Eh?'

He laughed again. 'One or two, I suppose. What do you do?'

'For a living? Oh — I'm — er — with computers. I work for

EDC. I expect you've heard of the Leo project? Well, I'm on that. Firm's sent me to Chelton on a course and I'm living in one of their flats here. Very nice, been redecorated six months ago. We take exams every so often; I hope to pass out in three months from now and take a post on the Gallipoli scheme in Ghana. It should be very interesting.'

'It sounds it. I don't know much about computers, I'm afraid.'

'Never mind. Come on, drink up. I don't know about you, but I'm all in favour of a spot of bed.' He smiled and stood up. Nicky wondered if he could slip away. Tom did not seem so attractive now; there was something rather aggressive about his manner. You heard such stories: casual pick-ups could be robbed, or beaten senseless, or murdered even. Suppose Tom were really odd and wanted to tie him up, or whip him?

They left the refreshment-room. 'Where's the car?' Tom shouted over the din of station noises. Nicky led the way to the car park. The station was busy; the London train was due to leave. People bustled about their ordinary business; an engine hissed; doors slammed and a guard blew his whistle. The hubbub reverberated and magnified under the great glass dome of Chelton station. Nicky felt helpless, the only person in this crowd whose actions were leading to danger, to disaster even. He wanted to run, leap on a train, but he knew he could not.

By the car Tom said, 'I'll drive. I know the way; it'll be quicker.'

'It's not insured for you.'

'Oh, it doesn't matter. I'm insured to drive any car.'

Nicky thought of the horror his mother would experience if she could guess that a total stranger had handled the steering-wheel of the new Marina. 'I shall drive it,' he said, firmly.

'Oh, fair enough. Carry on.' Nicky unlocked the door, and let Tom in on the passenger side. 'Drive down to the City Centre, and take the London Road. You know Watergate Street? I'll tell you where we go after that. Is it your car?' They set off down Station Approach.

'No. It's my mother's'. He wanted to boast that he owned it himself, but he was afraid Tom would not believe him. It was only since he had started teaching practice that his mother had allowed him to borrow the car regularly, and only then because there was no convenient bus service over the twelve miles to the school at Clemingham.

'How old are you, Nicky?'

'Nineteen.'

'Nineteen!' Tom sounded oddly disconcerted. 'I took you for

older.'

'Did you?' Nicky was surprised. 'Nobody else has ever done so. How old are you?'

'Oh, twenty-five. Turn right here, by the way. What do you teach, Nicky?'

'Divinity, mainly. And some music.'

'Music? I like music. We'll put on a record when we get in. I've got the new Beethoven symphony. Do you play any sport?'

'No. I'm not a games-player, I'm afraid.'

'You should be. It's fun. I play quite a bit of rugger myself, and some athletics.'

So he *was* a games-player. Nicky glanced sideways with a pang of desire; there would be fine muscles, a real man's physique under the clothes: everything that he lacked and yearned for. It was starting to rain. He switched on the windscreen wipers.

'What do you do?' Tom asked.

'Do?'

'In bed, I mean.'

'Oh.' Nicky considered. 'It depends.'

'I'm quite versatile myself. Are you versatile? What do you like doing best?'

Nicky was not sure what this really meant. 'I don't mind,' he said vaguely.

'We are going to have some fun, aren't we?' Tom leaned forward, worried. 'You aren't going to let me down, are you? I'm looking forward to a real sexy time now.'

'Of course. Of course. So am I.'

'Are you sure?' He still sounded anxious. 'When did you last have some fun?'

He thought. 'A fortnight ago, perhaps.'

'Well,' said Tom in a more relaxed tone, 'the best thing to do is to climb into bed and see. If we like it, we like it; I'll give you the phone number and you can come again. If not, no skin off anyone's nose, eh?'

'Yes, that's fine.'

'Have you been in that refreshment-room before?'

'No. Someone at college told me about it. That's why I was there.'

'It's pretty well-known, that refreshment-room. Pretty notorious. You want to watch out for yourself.' He stroked Nicky's left hand, touching the signet ring, easing it just a little up the third finger. 'That's a very expensive-looking ring you've got there,' he said.

'My mother gave it me last birthday. You think it looks expensive?'

'Isn't it, then?'

'I doubt if it's worth much.'

Tom rubbed at the condensation on the windscreen. 'We're nearly there,' he said. 'Keep on for a bit and take the third on the left.' He began to look about him as if he was not certain of the direction. He wiped the window on his left with the flat of his hand and peered out. 'It's all right, I know where we are. I was just looking round to see if there was anyone about. It looks a bit odd, doesn't it, if you take a stranger in, a bloke, at this time of day, and he leaves an hour later. I don't want anyone to think there's anything like that going on, even though we are — here, this one. Turn left here. Oh no, you can't; it's a no-entry. You'll have to take the next one.'

Nicky steered the car into a narrow one-way street. It was a part of Chelton he did not know very well, the Sheffield district. The street had tall warehouses on either side.

'Pull in here,' said Tom. 'Here, I tell you!' he said sharply, as Nicky was about to overshoot the parking-space. The car just fitted in neatly between two lorries. Nicky switched the engine off, and they heard the patter of the rain on the glass. The windscreen quickly became blurred.

'My flat's in the block on the corner,' said Tom. 'You can't see it from your side. There's a porter there, a caretaker. I'm just wondering what he'll think when he sees us. I can't afford to take risks being in a company flat; I've got a career to think of just like you have. I mean, if you got up to anything with one of your boys it would be an awful risk, wouldn't it?' He shifted about uneasily, sucking at a broken finger-nail. 'I tell you what. We'll buy a bottle of scotch and take it in. If he sees us then, well, it's just two lads going up for a drink; pubs aren't open yet, so he'll take it as normal.'

'But if the pubs are shut, you won't be — '

'There's a grocer over the way; I know the old woman there. We'll go halves, shall we?' Nicky looked doubtful. 'Surely you want a drink, don't you?'

'Yes. All right.'

'Have you got change of a fiver? The old girl's always short of change.'

'I don't think so.' Nicky pulled out the contents of his inside pocket. There were old letters, his driving licence, his diary, a recorded delivery receipt for a parcel, a cheque-book, his school time-table, and pound notes, loose. He did not possess a wallet.

'You haven't got much there,' Tom remarked. 'Don't you ever carry more money than that? How much do you have there?'

'Two or three pounds, isn't it? I wasn't counting.'

'How much is it?' Tom persisted. 'I want to know.'

'Two or three pounds. I said so!'

'Are you sure?'

'Yes! What business is it of yours anyway?'

'Now, Nicky, don't lose your temper.' Tom laid a restraining hand on his arm. 'There's absolutely no need to lose your temper. I'm just interested in — in matters of finance, that's all. Have you any dirty postcards in with that lot?'

'No, I have not.' Nicky began to feel alarmed. In front towered the blank grey doors of the pantechnicon; to the right was a warehouse wall. There was no escape.

'I don't like chaps with dirty postcards, see? I once got involved with one and there was a bit of bother with the police. What's that sticking out?' He touched a corner of one of the pound notes.

'Mind your own business.' Nicky tried to put his things back in his inside pocket, but immediately two strong hands, the envied games-player's hands, grabbed his wrist and twisted. There was a short struggle and Tom was left holding Nicky's possessions.

'Give them back!' Nicky shouted.

'I will. Just keep calm. I only want to make sure there are no dirty postcards here.' He extracted three pound notes and screwed them up tightly in his left fist. Everything else he dropped onto the floor. Nicky sat still, terrified; Tom was obviously much stronger and would easily win another scuffle.

'Now the silver.' Nicky's heart sank. Only that morning he had collected in 10p pieces from 2B. He was going to take them to the zoo in London, and this was their fare money. The children were very excited about it and most of them had paid at the first available opportunity. A trip to London by coach! And in school time, too! Nicky's right-hand pocket was weighed down with the tokens of their enthusiasm.

'I haven't got any silver.'

'I said silver!!' Tom bellowed, and he banged his fist on the steering-wheel. His breathing was fast, excited, and his eyes were two small blazes of ice-blue.

'But — '

'Oh come here.' He leaned across, thrust his hand into Nicky's pocket and wrenched out the contents. He whistled with surprise at the handful of money.

'You lied to me, Nicky,' he said, hurt. 'You lied to me. You said you hadn't any silver. There's at least ten quid here.'

'Give it back,' Nicky pleaded. 'Do give it back, please. It's not my money. It's the children's.' His voice faltered as he thought of their eager faces. 'I'm taking them to the zoo and it's their coach money.'

'You ought to have more consideration for them. Walking into a place like that refreshment-room with all their cash on you! You ought to be ashamed of yourself, Nicky. Don't you feel ashamed of yourself?' The money clinked as it dropped into his pocket.

'No.'

'You're a pretty poor schoolmaster, Nicky. Standing up in front of a class and wanting sex with boys, lusting for them! People like you should be done away with. Liquidated. Why don't you pull yourself together? You're young enough. Why not make a fresh start? Teach some girls for a change.'

'I do teach girls.' He was having to justify himself: it was preposterous. Yet he did not know how to answer the charges. 'I do teach girls,' he repeated, wanting to be understood.

'But you teach boys as well, don't you? You said so yourself. And they make you feel so randy you have to run to places like that refreshment-room the moment school's ended!' His voice rose in indignation. 'It's revolting. Deplorable.' He shook his head.

'But I told you, I've never been there before.'

'It doesn't matter. If it wasn't there you would go somewhere else; there's plenty of places like that. Come now, aren't you ashamed of yourself?'

Nicky bowed his head. 'No.'

'You've doubtless got a wife and children too. Don't you ever think of them — '

'Me, married? I'm not married. I'm a student.' It was as if, for a fleeting moment, Tom had started off on the wrong gramophone record.

'You live at home, do you? Well, why not think about your mother sometimes, eh? Think of what she would have to suffer if she ever found out.'

'I do think about that. Often.'

'For Christ's sake do something about it then, Nicky! Look at me. I'm a con man and a crook and I've been in prison. And what are you? A homosexual schoolmaster. Now which of us, honestly, is worse? Eh?'

Tom half-opened the car door.

'Think about what I've said.' It was almost fatherly, a schoolmaster's advice. 'And make a fresh start.'

'Give me back some of that money,' Nicky pleaded. 'It's not mine. What am I going to say — '

'That's your problem. Anyway I haven't taken it all; there's still some left. I wouldn't leave a bloke skint.'

Nicky felt in his pocket and pulled out three 5p pieces.

'There you are, see? I'm as good as my word. *I* don't tell lies.'

'Please,' Nicky begged.

'Oh, all right.' His voice was grudging, disgusted. 'Here's 10p. No — why should I give you anything at all? You've got enough.' He might have used the same tone with a tramp who had asked for the price of a cup of tea. 'It's time we ended this game,' he said. 'You gambled and you lost.' He smiled, and his face looked pleasant, frank. 'So long.'

He got out and slammed the door. As Nicky started the car Tom turned and waved, still smiling, as if he were saying good-bye to a friend.

Nicky drove home, stunned, hardly seeing the traffic. The coins danced in front of his eyes, the windscreen wipers swathing through them; Tom's bright eyes laughed and the wipers swished off his head. Each swash sound as they moved back and forth across the glass said 'Bastard . . . bastard . . . bastard . . . '

CORRESPONDENCE

by Simon Burt

> Every person is like thousands
> of books. New, reprinting, in
> stock, out of stock, fiction, non-
> fiction, poetry, rubbish. The
> lot. Different every day. One's
> lucky to be able to put his hand
> on the one that's wanted, let
> alone know it.
>
> Russel Hoban

The summer of 1976 was a bad time for me. It was very hot and
London is not the place to be in a heat wave. There was little for
me to do except sit at my desk in my basement in Sussex Square,
writing scripts that nobody wanted to read, waiting for my wife to
divorce me. I guess I'm what you'd call a passive, a re-active person
at the best of times. I take my cue from other people. I behave as
they would expect or like, or according to my idea of what they
would expect or like. And this, as I discovered, was not only
driving my wife crazy, but was aggravated by the heat into a sort of
inertia, a surrender. We still lived together, my wife and I. We still
shared the same bed. But it was becoming increasingly obvious
that this state of affairs wasn't going to continue. And I could do
nothing about it. As I said, I'm a re-active sort of person. I treat
people the way they treat me. I take what I'm offered. And if my
wife was going to spend days without breaking the silence, so was
I. If she was going to ease the strain by taking the odd stranger to
bed, so was I. It had happened before, and we had weathered it.
This time, though, I could see that we weren't going to, and I
watched the process with paralysis, taking refuge in other people's
stories — I scripted three books that summer; the scripts are still
in my desk; I haven't even typed them out — and patiently

unsticking my shirt from my back, or when it got even hotter, my back from the leather chair.

I should I suppose be more clear, tell you more about what was going on between my wife and me, give examples. But this story's not about that, and that's not how I see stories anyway. As a matter of fact, she did leave me at the end of October, and it wasn't until our divorce was finalised that I even thought about how much I loved her and was going to miss her. But none of that comes into this story. I just mentioned it to give some idea of the background.What really matters is the passivity, the re-activeness for lack of a better word, the inertia. And the heat. It made everything like a dream, like living in a sluggish hallucination. It was a freak summer.

Occasionally, however, I did manage to drag myself about. I'd walk for a while in the park, drop in to the pub, chat with whoever of my wife's friends came by. I didn't see much of my own friends, but then I don't have many. Most of our friends were my wife's friends, as I discovered when I went through my address book after the divorce. It was on one of my expeditions to the park that I met Larry, who sticks in my mind as the strangest ingredient of that strange summer, encapsulates it in my memory. We met in the Italian garden. He made some comment on the number of cigarette cartons as opposed to the number of ducks. We had some sort of desultory conversation about heat and air-conditioning, and after about half an hour I took him home to bed. The night before, my wife had spent with the Japanese pop singer she married when she was through with me, so I felt, if not justified, at least not guilty about Larry. It wasn't a success. It was too hot for more than a functional fumble, but I gave him my telephone number when he left, and told him to keep in touch, which is something I don't normally do; so I must have felt there was some potential there worth pursuing.

He called me the next day with an invitation to tea. He lived alone in a tiny, empty flat in Evelyn Gardens. After tea we went to bed again, and this time it was better, as it often is with casual sex, if you can make the effort to go along with it. Next day I called him, and after that there was daily communication of some sort or another. I called him. He called me. I went to his flat. He came to mine. My wife met him, and was bowled over. He was a very charming guy. Witty, polite and all that. Great fun to be with. We spent more time laughing than anything else. He was relaxing to be with, and of course he brought out the same thing in me. Everything was going fine. I even felt that I was getting on better with my wife, until I got the letter. And now I'd better try and make you see just how much that was a surprise.

Despite the impression I must have given so far, I'm not all that interested in casual sex. If it goes badly, and with me it often does, it's simply boring. And when it goes well it just leaves me with an increased appetite. It leaves too many questions unanswered, and generally speaking it doesn't satisfy me at all. With Larry, though, it was different. As I said, he was a nice guy, relaxed, carefree, easy. He took me out of myself. He made my life easy too, at least for the four or five weeks before he sent the letter. I became for a while what I've always wanted to be, an immediate person, the sort of person who can live in the present, and be satisfied, happy to do so. I mean, I usually agonise over the smallest decision. In fact, I postpone making it until the situation has gone so far that the decision is made for me. It took me so long to make up my mind to visit the Chinese exhibition, for instance, that they took it off before I got there. And that's typical. That happens to me all the time. But with Larry it didn't happen. We went out. To plays, concerts, films. We did all the usual London things that I somehow never get round to doing, and certainly wouldn't have done that summer, because of the inertia and the heat. We ended up having the sort of relationship that I often think is the best there is. We were good friends who went to bed together, and it was light-hearted and beautiful. Spontaneous. And if that's too embarrassing, too mawkish for you, I can't help it. That's the way it was. I don't apologise. But then there was the letter. And now I've mentioned it a couple of times I suppose I'd better tell you what it said. I still have it, and the other two letters he sent me. I've kept them because they still confuse me, even now. I still don't understand them at all. I don't suppose you will either, but then this story isn't about understanding.

Dear Michael,

Shyness is a dreadful disease. I read somewhere that it locks all emotion to the pit of the stomach, all expression to the tip of the tongue. Well that's a fine saying. All I know is that shyness is a prison. A prison I've spent my life trying to break out of, but with no success. I'm under a life sentence. I can't get out. I can only pretend, more or less skilfully, not to be shy, and hope that one day I'll maybe fool myself, succeed in deceiving myself as I deceive others. And I do deceive them, don't I? You asked me the other day if I liked being with you. We were both a bit drunk, so maybe you don't remember. Most people would have answered with an unhesitating Yes, and that would have been that. The truth would have been out. But I, being me and shy, said Isn't it obvious? and you said No, it isn't. I made some silly remark about keeping things secret, about not stating anything until it was obvious. Some such rubbish. Well, I find I can't wait. And it bloody well should be obvious, you unobservant bastard. If it wasn't then, it must be now. Anyway, that's what this letter is all about. Certain things I can't say, but I can write them, so here goes.

I was going to write that I was falling in love with you, but it seems silly to set out on a confession with a half truth. I'm not falling in love with you. I've been through that. I love you. All the time.

Well, I've said it. I hope you don't mind. For years now I've felt that I was never going to love anyone again, and I have been, or so I thought, happy within that limitation. It's amazing, isn't it? for how long one can survive in a state of virtual anaesthesia. Many times when I've been ill I've refused to go to bed. I've walked around, hazy with fever, and adjusted to it. It's only after I've recovered that I realise how different it all was. Every state that one is in seems natural as long as one is in it. And now, only now, I know how unhappy the last few years have been. How I have been longing for love, as a sick man longs for recovery, but just didn't know that was what I wanted. I was insulated, I discover, by my fear. If my loving you scares you half as much as it scares me then boy are you scared! I know, none better, the pain love brings, the sleeplessness, the fever, the hope. I've tried to live without hope, and until I met you I think I succeeded. You have given me back hope, and it's a mixed blessing. Mixed because, if hope has returned, peace has vanished. Still, all in all, at least I know I'm alive again. And so, despite the usual crying to sleep, or worse, the fruitless questioning of my bleak moonlit pillow — don't be deluded by the distancing irony. The pain is genuine and complete — I'm glad I love you, and I'm glad I've told you I love you.

Two pages is long enough for a love letter. More and I shall repeat myself, do what I spend most of my day doing anyway, say I love you, I love you, I love you, over and over, and that would be a bore. I must just say one more thing, though, and that is that I know you hate demands, and you must know that I'm not making any. I haven't yet, I'm not now, and I won't. I know that's easy to say, and it's easy to disbelieve too. You'll just have to take my word for it.

And here The Letter ends. Just Love Larry would be best, wouldn't it? So

Love,
Larry

I guess I must be unobservant, because it was a surprise. I don't quite know how to explain the effect it had on me. It was just so unlike Larry. It was disturbing. I felt trapped, betrayed, and confused. I'm not sure why. It should have been good. I should have felt glad. But I didn't. I felt as if someone had accumulated all the heat of the summer and heaved it onto my shoulders like a sack. I felt really bad. Guilty, I suppose, more than anything else. And angry at my mistake, at having so serenely missed the point. I spent half an hour or so pacing up and down saying How was I to know? And then I went to bed and slept. I always do when things get too much for me. I wrap myself into the foetal position, chew on my thumbnail, and sleep.

My wife woke me. She reminded me that we were giving a dinner party, for Larry among others, and said maybe I'd like to come and help her get it ready. I sat on the edge of the bed for a while, still thinking about Larry's letter, and when I went through to the kitchen I found her leaning her head against the wall. I put my arms round her shoulders and she turned and held me.

'Chibo playing you up, is he?' I said. 'The pug-faced pop idol.'

'I hate this,' she said. 'We can't go on like this.'

'No,' I said. 'I know we can't. I'll help you with dinner.'

And I went into the dining-room to lay the table. We didn't speak again till Chibo arrived, then Larry and the others, and the party started. It went very well, mainly due to Larry. He behaved just as usual. I looked very hard, before I gave up and got drunk, but I couldn't detect the smallest change. He talked and laughed just as usual, and soon everyone else was talking and laughing too, as if we were all happy people, and I knew for a fact that at least four of us were not that. But it made no difference. We all had a good time. And I didn't have a chance to say anything to Larry about the letter till he was leaving, by which time I was so drunk, and so confused, I must have messed it up. If I was confused before, I was more so now. If I couldn't connect the Larry I knew with the man who had written that letter, it was impossibly strange to see him now, behaving so exactly as he normally did, so exactly as if he hadn't written the letter, so exactly as if he were the sort of person who wouldn't have written such a letter, even after he had done so and knew that I had received it. I swear there wasn't the smallest difference. I walked him to the door when he decided to go, and said 'I got your letter' on the doorstep. He looked at me as if he didn't understand what I was saying, then his expression changed to a look of slight surprise, as if I'd made an error of taste. 'Yes?' he said. Then he smiled, and said goodbye, and went. I returned to the party, but it wasn't the same after Larry had gone, and soon broke up.

When I woke up the next morning the lethargy was back. I sat at my desk all day till Larry phoned about six. We chatted for a few minutes, still as if nothing had happened, and arranged to meet the next day. Then things carried on much as before, but with two important differences, both on my side. My inertia was back. Except for the times when I was with him I couldn't do anything. The laundry built up in the bag, till my wife cracked and did it herself, on a night when she was supposed to be going out with Chibo, to underline my dereliction. And I stopped phoning Larry. Instead he phoned me. It became a ritual. Every day after he got back from work at five thirty, he called me and we talked. More often than not, but less often than before, we arranged to meet. The initiative was all on his side. But we did meet. And we went out together, and went to bed together, as apparently light-heartedly and spontaneously as before. Of course 'apparently' is the key adverb. We both knew he had written the letter, although he certainly wasn't going to talk about it. One day, three or four weeks later, I was out when he called, and I woke up the next morning to find another letter, delivered by hand. It made even less sense than the first.

Dear Michael,

It's the middle of the night and I can't sleep. This is no unusual thing these days, but tonight, because you weren't in when I phoned, it's worse. I'm acutely conscious of telephoning you all the time, and I've got to get this straight. I'm sorry if it's a bore, but I've got to ask you a very important question. Don't worry, though. I'm only going to ask it once.

I told you I loved you and meant it. I thought it would make me feel better but it didn't. I love you so much that it hurts. And I'm making myself ill. I can't work, or sleep, for wondering what, if anything, you feel for me. That's why I keep telephoning. Sometimes it makes me feel better, sometimes worse. But not speaking to you, as I found out tonight, is worse. So I've got to ask the question I swore I wouldn't ask. I think maybe you don't know what you feel. I think maybe you haven't thought about it. But please, my dear, do think about it a bit, and find some way of letting me know, somehow, sometimes, what you feel.

I'm sorry if this sounds a bit hysterical, but I live alone and have hours to brood in. I'm scared to death of pain, and right now it hurts so bad that I'm prepared to do anything, even force myself to ask questions like this one, to stop it. So if all this does bore the pants off you, please tell me, and I can carry on the fight to get my emotions under control.

Love,
Larry

He called at eleven o'clock that morning to say he'd taken the day off work, and we met for lunch. After lunch we went for a walk in the park, and to a photographic exhibition at the Serpentine Gallery. We talked about the things we usually talked about. His work, mine. His plans, mine. His friends, mine. Nothing about anything even remotely connected with love. Then we went back to his flat, went to bed, went to a movie, and separated to go home. We met again the next day, and almost daily thereafter as before. His letter wasn't mentioned. He turned the subject if I even got close to mentioning it. It was all very strange. I couldn't handle it. I mean, here was this man sending me passionate and tormented letters — or at least that's how they seemed, though admittedly I've got small experience of love letters; Larry's are the only ones I've ever received — and not showing any sign of what he professed, which made it that much more frantic, somehow. Wouldn't you be confused? I didn't know what to do, and, as always, I played it his way. And this carried on right the way through to the end of October, when my wife left to live with Chibo.

I arrived home one day from one of my dragging walks in the park to find Chibo sitting over a sherry in the dining-room, and a pile of suitcases in the hall. I thought at first that he was moving in, till I recognised the suitcases and knew my wife was moving out. So I poured myself a sherry too, and sat making polite conversation with Chibo until my wife came in from the bedroom and said it was time to go. They took the cases out to Chibo's car and drove off. Half an hour later the doorbell rang, and there was my wife on the doorstep saying:

'You don't mind, do you? You can't mind. Say you don't mind. I mean, you've got Larry.'

I could have told her that this wasn't any way to see our relation-ship, that relationships don't work in that commercial sort of way, that in every separation there is one partner who falls on his feet and one who falls on his ass, and I knew damn well who'd fallen on his ass in this one. I could have told her that I didn't have Larry anyway, or didn't know whether I had him or not, any more than he did, and it wasn't relevant either. But there didn't seem any point. So I said nothing, and waited for her to go away. I didn't want to make her parting any easier for her than she had made it. And I wasn't going to have a grand renunciation scene, certainly not on the doorstep. So I didn't say anything, and she went to live with Chibo, where she still lives, as far as I know. I called Larry for the first time in weeks, and we met for a drink. I didn't tell him my wife had gone, but he must have guessed, because he sent me the third letter.

Dear Michael,

I've been telling myself that the relationship we both so desperately want we could have with each other, but it isn't true, you know. This is to say goodbye. This is it. The point of any friendship is that it should be enjoyable, that it should give joy, and if it doesn't then it must stop. And our friendship sure as hell isn't giving me any joy, so I'm going to stop it. Give me a couple of months and I won't love you any more. It will be a bad couple of months. It will be like tearing my arm off at the shoulder without anaesthetic. But it has to be done. It's not easy to explain why, but I guess I owe it to you, and to myself, to try. My life has turned into a continual dialogue with you. Everything I do or see doesn't exist unless or until I share it with you. When I'm not with you I just sit doing nothing except thinking how much I love you, being nothing except in love with you. Every action I make is haunted with memories of when I did it with you. I can't put on a shirt without crying, because the last time I wore it I was with you. The only way I can cope with my love for you is by not thinking of you, taking away the root of the obsession, and though I don't want to do that, though the prospect of doing that fills me with horror, that is what I'm going to have to do. On balance the pain of being without you is less than the pain of being with you, and has the edge because it is at least temporary. After a little time I shall learn to live without my arm. But living with you would be just pure hell, not for any reason or fault of yours, but because I love you too much. Do you understand? Even if you loved me back, which though I know you like me, I know don't, I couldn't bear it. Love, though in itself not a disaster — but maybe in this case it is a disaster because you don't love me, and I'm not the sort of person who can be happy just to be in love, with no prospect of return, as some possibly nobler people can — Love brings with it such a heightened exacerbation of the senses and emotions as to be in the long run unendurable. The storms are very fierce, and I have, with a fear and reluctance too great for adverbs, decided to withdraw myself from them. I feel like a visitor from another planet. The simplest things are strange to me. A button fell off my jacket a week ago. I couldn't bring myself to sew it on till yesterday, and even when I did it took half an hour, my hand was shaking so much, my mind was so full of you. It's as if I were too wide awake on one level, seeing and hearing more than other people, because my love for you has woken me up, and on another level faster asleep, wading through dreams of you. Oh dear, I knew I'd make a botch of explaining it all. But I've done the best I can. Please try and understand. Excess of happiness is unhappiness. Excess of both is misery.

Anyway I've made up my mind. I'm not going to love you any more. Don't, please, blame yourself. It's not your fault. To be brutal, it has little to do with you. If you loved me back it would only make it worse. So for the last time,

Love,
Larry

It would make more sense if I could say that I didn't see him again, but I did. That evening he called me, and we went to a movie. He behaved just as always. We talked, we laughed, we went to bed. And often again afterwards till he left for New York the following January. I still don't know what the hell it was all about. I moved from Sussex Square to a smaller flat, a flat for one, in Ladbroke Grove. I still get letters from him, but those I don't keep. They are ordinary letters, full of New York gossip, the sort of letters friends write to each other. We haven't had a hot summer since.

THE DANCE

by Sam Green

The phone call was answered, as always, with hope. No, it was not the joker. It was a real phone call.

Sam lies; he hasn't really forgotten about the disco. 'Of course I don't mind doing the door.'

But he must not sound too relieved, too eager to get out of the house, to do something, something for them at the disco. He says he'll come when some telly programme or other he is half-watching has finished. 'No, if it is important I'll come right away.' Good. He'll have something to do. He doesn't like discos as it means hanging around.

Hanging round at discos is like cottaging with flashing lights, only much less anonymous. Much more self-conscious.

But you don't have to make the effort when you do the door – you're an activist. Committed. Like addressing election envelopes for the revolution.

The cold bone-chilling weather was not the climate for washing in. With wandering slowness the cleansing lotion was applied. Moisturising cream rubbed in, rubbed out. Sam should have looked after himself better. At forty . . . thirty-eight actually, but what is two years?

The room is too cold to change in. But it is my home. It's nice having your own house and owning it outright and sharing it with other people.

But why did Sam have the coldest room, the small box room where one could not have a fire?

I don't want to waste energy and am not materialistic in any way.

Yes, Sam does occasionally wear a Friends of the Earth badge, but he did not have his roof properly slated, let alone properly lagged.

A university wife said that Sam could not fulfil himself in normal ways so he did it by patronising people — the people he had taken to share his house with him. That was why, she once told him, he surrounded himself with people weaker than himself — 'thieves and scroungers' — why there had been trouble, the police always calling, the . . .

No that's not really true. It's political, to do with working for an alternative to the nuclear family, finding a different way of living, an active parallel against homelessness.

Oh God, where were we? Oh yes, changing in the cold. Or not changing. I don't want to change to go to the disco.

Was it because of the cold, or was it because Sam had no competitive dancing-clothes in the wardrobe? No natty suits. No tight trousers. The only snow-resistant (i.e. without holes in the soles) shoes were factory boots.

My own unique protest. Some form of living parody – look scruffy against youthism.

My mother always said I was scruffy and she feels ashamed of me. We are wandering a bit in our old age, aren't we? And I have just told them I will hurry.

The real reasons for grabbing that handful of tatty jewellery from an untidy windowsill in an even dirtier room were easier to explain.

It is political. It is to annoy. It is to show the 'bit bairns' that there is still some life left in the old queen.

Sam and Gerry! Sam still loves Gerry Miller and Gerry Miller wore jewellery 'politically' as a demonstration against straight society. No, it was to show he was different from them. Better. An angel.

Sam did not love him because of the jewellery.

Or do I? He isn't bad-looking, I suppose, but – oh well, I fancied people who were younger . . . He is so powerful, so gentle, a vision of life as it should be. Gay.

They just sat there eating beans on benches. And Sam spoke to Gerry. Of course, replied Gerry, he had come to the Gay Anarchist conference for political reasons — not the booze and the dancing. And Sam was put firmly in his place. They were to meet again.

But now I . . . am in Durham.

A city with a cathedral, a university with a preponderance of ex-public school students, set in a heavy industrial area ruled by a city council that has only one Conservative councillor, but whose council has the desire to Bring Back the Birch to make the city safe at night.

No, it is not just the lack of a coloured population that makes it different from Bradford.

Until recently Sam had been a councillor in the small-town city where most people knew everyone. The first Liberal councillor the town had had, and the first admitted homosexual in Britain to hold elected office — or so he said.

People I've not met before still remember and occasionally (very occasionally) say 'I remember you from that programme.' They usually come from London.

All because of that election a decade ago. At the time it happened I found when I went into Newcastle's piss-elegant Eldon people looked at me and pointed. The uninhibited said 'Hello.'

Previously Sam had hardly dared sneak in, felt embarrassed even before anyone who looked turned away. (He was no chicken even then, and had never been desirable property.) It was rare for someone to talk.

Cottaging is less embarrassing, and at least there is contact through the under-wall notes.

It is not winning the election that is noticed. The local weekly did not even mention the 'gay angle'. It was a year later when someone in London decided it would make a good subject for a World in Action tv programme - a half-hour feature at peak viewing time.

Just as Sam had thought putting he was gay on his election address would ensure he lost, so he thought the tv programme would be an embarrassing sacrifice for the cause. Funny how you can get people wrong, isn't it Sam?

I finger the jewellery in my pockets. My pace is quick, not because I am late but because I am always wary when the pubs are open in Durham.

But at Bradford . . .

I first went to Bradford to watch - the time 200 people were arrested for sitting down and stopping the traffic. But just like the naughty boy who doesn't believe in fairies is shown in all good Enid Blyton fairy stories the path that leads to Fairyland, so when I walked from Manningham to Bradford Centre that path was opened to me.

It would have been unnatural not to go. It was so restful walking through the streets protesting against the National Front by singing 'Teddy Bears' Picnic' with an assortment of gays dressed as carnival animals - led of course by a beautiful Teddy Bear.

The rule of Law and Order. How could I not sit down and be arrested along with 200 others, many from local CHE groups who like me had never been on a demo before? It was so lovely.

After twelve hours in a police cell your mind wanders in heavenly directions. It didn't seem like a put-off when a leather-clad university lecturer I was cuddling said 'No, not in here. Not in a police cell.'

And appearing in court along with 200 others sentenced to £20 fines over a two-day period. Standing in the dock with the back end of an elephant. Well what could be more relevant – jumble sales and council committees?

Years after that demo Sam became a temporary part of the Bradford scene, and then left. And returned for another demo in Bradford.

One of us had been arrested for 'offences against a minor' and we were protesting against his 'forced and false' confession. But it was all so different. So unnatural. The banners and slogans instead of the songs and the Teddy Bear.

Why should such evil be allowed in our country? Why should they be allowed to flaunt themselves so? Why couldn't the authorities leave us alone and only air their prejudices in private?

> And if I start looking behind me,
> And start retracing my tracks,
> Please remind me to remind you
> We said we would not look back.

As Sam walks through the streets he has the dance to look forward to. The cobbled streets, the manly cathedral with the chocolate-box market place complete with reproduction street-furniture. His town. The town he is part of.

Yes, Sam the tatty is safely pocketed out of sight. You look no different from them. The drunken youths who recognise you and shout 'poof' in the streets.

Gerry Miller from Bradford did look different. The gentleness of strength, and the vulnerability of certainty. The right you must follow but don't. The man who never plays man's games — straight games.

I never did mean to let Gerry know – as that would spoil it. It always does. I just looked cow-eyed, when we were together for three months. But one night I burst into drunken tears, sobs. 'I can't help it, don't blame me.' He held me closer and said 'I know. I've always known.' We kissed. I cried. I was drunk.

He was that kind of person – he felt guilty because he could not reciprocate. He felt it wrong only to be able to offer affection.

Unlike Gerry I do not look like a poof, not now as I walk through Durham. But still they shout at me 'Sammy's a poof'. Gerry would have shouted at them. But this old queen is growing old. When you get old you get tired.

I had been Peter Pan in Bradford only a few months ago. But not tonight. I knew they would shout. I expected it. I am used to them. I always walk quickly through the streets of Durham when the drunks are around.

I did not have any audition. No audition. They were from Bradford. They remembered me from the demonstration and the anarchist conference.

They were against professionalism and were touring with a play. Gays expressing gay problems. What I was expressing was a rather nice, rather liberal, rather old-fashioned, sexually closeted Trade Unionist who could remember the General Strike. He was called Sid.

I had been the oldest at the conference and one of the oldest arrested nearly a decade before. The policeman told me I should have grown out of this sort of thing. But touring I was young. Yes, anyone can be Peter Pan with Don, Charles, Colin, Youseff, Frank and Gerry. Together. Alone one is old.

Seated by the door checking tickets for the dance he puts on the tat. It would put off the straights coming in for 'an experience' or the out-for-a-laugh City males.

We kissed on meeting. Not just a kiss, but a holding touch. And now I am sitting by the door checking tickets.

Touring. Rowing about real issues. Should gays have anything to do with straights? Talks in isolation solve problems.

The local groups we visited would say 'What's it like being an actor? You mean you've never acted before?' And that was after I fluffed my lines, as I did every night.

And I am sitting at the door wearing tatty old-fashioned jewellery – just like we did in Bradford. What is liberation?

Yes, everything is alright. The disco already made a profit and there would be a pound or two left to send to Northern Ireland.

Should I have come home? I knew when I got out of the van at the end of the tour it was over. I was ending it.

Surely I could build on my experience in the town where until I resigned 'to become an actor' I had been a councillor. Home. Me.

The dance is really so sedate. So different from . . . No different from straight.

No Rational Person could find better behaviour at a strawberry tea run by Conservatives.

People rational? 'Do you think I'll be alright going through that lot?' asked a university cleaner. She had that I-know-you smile, and I who have a hopeless memory for faces suspected she had been at one time one of the people who supported me as the councillor who spoke up for 'people like us'.

People rational? I keep getting instructed 'Trouble from the Town', 'Town Yobs Again', 'Keep Them Out'. Who is who? And who is going away in three years' time? The yobs and the hooligans? Or the educated university elite?

But it does not really matter. At one pound fifty a head they do not want to come in. A Rational Decision.

POOFS!

BUM BOYS!

BOTTY MEN!

QUEERS! scream the youths.

Are people rational, Sam? Some toilets outside the place we were dancing in are damaged. 'Did you lot do this?' the porter asks the dancers. What would have happened if we were heterosexuals with the queens screaming outside?

'Someone's car's been damaged!' Aggro flows from within. Physical anger for us. Against them. Confrontation. Shouting swearing screaming. Good.

This only queen is angry. As he walks home through the town he is proud of wearing his jewellery — in all its glory. Drunk and carrying a broken glass in his pocket just in case.

Back home to bed. To sleep — alone.

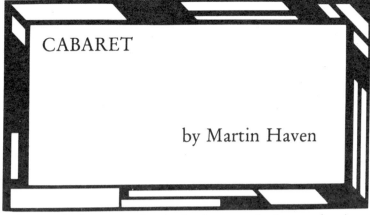

CABARET

by Martin Haven

The nice-looking man in the leather coat had seemed quite interested but hadn't bothered to hang around for very long; undeterred by the weather, he had soon left the shelter of the doorway and gone off out of sight round the corner.

Though not out of mind; Malcolm continued to brood on what he saw as lost opportunity as he remained huddled in the entrance to the Underground, watching the rain cascade down onto the shining streets outside. 'It would start raining now of course. Just my luck. I expect he wanted me to follow him, but how can I?' he grieved, feeling both wronged and angered by his plight. He scowled down at his watch, saw the time and swore loudly; a passing middle-aged woman glared her disapproval and he sneered back in defiance. With a look of contempt she stepped away from him into the wet darkness to hurry off down the street, her smartly-shod feet picking their way carefully through the puddles on the uneven pavement, her showy outfit and hairdo protected by a large umbrella. 'Stupid old cow,' he muttered after her, and moved away from the doorway to cast yet another impatient glance around the station entrance; he raised his eyes to heaven at the sight of Howard turning out his pockets at the ticket barrier, blocking the flow of people surging up from the escalator behind him.

'Where the bloody hell have you been?' he demanded, when Howard, having finally found his ticket, had emerged intact from the angry hordes of passengers and greeted him apologetically.

'I'm sorry I'm late Malcolm, I got held up at work,' said Howard, struggling to unfasten the umbrella he was carrying.

'Held up? You ought to be strung up.' Malcolm snatched the umbrella from him and opened it with ease. 'Do you realise how long I've been waiting here for you? Forty-five minutes. Three-quarters of a bloody hour.' He marched out of the tube station and walked quickly away, leaving Howard to run after him through the pouring rain.

'I'm sorry Malcolm,' repeated Howard, catching up with but still excluded from the umbrella that Malcolm kept held away from him. 'I tried to get here on time but there was some problem with returned books and the library didn't close till late. And really, you needn't have waited. I mean, it was very nice of you, but I could have made my own way to the pub.'

'Needn't have waited?' Malcolm glared at him accusingly. 'How the hell could I have gone out in this downpour and ruined my new haircut I've just spent so much money on? What did you expect me to do — wear a sou'wester?' He laughed scornfully. 'Of course I wouldn't have bothered to wait if I'd only had this umbrella, which you had to go and leave at the library yesterday. I'll never lend you anything again.'

Howard mumbled further apologies as he splashed his way through puddles in an unsuccessful attempt to equal Malcolm's long, impatient strides. He'd forgotten Malcolm was going to have his hair cut earlier that evening, and was sorry for forgetting, and said so.

'Don't worry, it'd be asking too much to expect you to remember anyone else's appointments when you can't even keep your own. I said half-past eight you were supposed to meet me and where the bloody hell were you?' Malcolm threw out this question while dashing across the road just as the red man flashed onto the pedestrian signal opposite; behind him Howard hesitated and was separated by the rush of traffic. He stood and waited for the lights to change, a small bedraggled figure on the kerb, watching Malcolm recede into the distance on the other side of the street; by the time he'd finally caught up, they were already at the doorway of the pub and Malcolm no longer wanted to know the reasons for his lateness.

'I've wasted enough bloody time this evening as it is without having to hear the saga of your journey here as well.' He shook out the sopping umbrella and unzipped his denim jacket, checking his reflection in the glass of the door before making his entrance. 'The least you can do is get me a drink,' he called over his shoulder as he pushed his way into the packed interior. 'I'll see you over by the bar in a minute — after standing so long in that freezing tube station I'm dying for a pee.'

Steeling himself, Howard followed him through the mock-Victorian doorway to meet the usual sea of faces waiting within, stationed ready to examine and pass critical judgment on each new arrival. As Malcolm disappeared across the room, Howard excused himself through the crowd and made slow, unsteady progress to the bar. The pub was very busy tonight, as it was Friday and the start of the weekend, and he was soon forced to stop short behind a tall, fat man dressed in leather and a short, thick beard, who gave him the briefest of cursory glances before continuing to peer hopefully round the rest of the assembly as he too waited in passive resignation to be served. At the head of the queue was a middle-aged American, squeezed unsuccessfully into a brightly-checked shirt and blue denims. His dark brown hair-dye was picked out maliciously by the harsh fluorescent lights above the bar as he stood with bent head and bowed shoulders, fumbling for change to pay the impatient barman, who then went off to serve a friend at the other end of the bar, leaving the rest of them still waiting.

'Considering the price of the drinks here, you'd think we'd get better service. It's always the same. I don't know why we put up with it, I really don't,' muttered a disgruntled voice somewhere to Howard's right, and several heads nodded in agreement, but they were still all standing there quietly putting up with it when Malcolm re-emerged some ten minutes later.

'Haven't you even got served yet? Howard, you're hopeless, you really are! Here, give me the money and *I'll* get the drinks. I might have known if I wanted a drink I'd have to fetch it myself in the end.'

With accustomed skill Malcolm pushed his way smartly to the front of the queue and had soon attracted the barman's attention; five minutes later, as they stood pressed against the wall in the crush, he was sipping his lager and looking around him with a satisfied smile.

'Quite a bit of talent here tonight,' he commented approvingly. 'There was a *very* nice bloke flashing at me in the loo. I thought he'd followed me out but I can't seem to see him. I think I'll go and have a look in the back bar in case he went in there. It'd be a pity to lose him, he had a nice cock.'

Squeezing himself through the packed bodies, Malcolm threaded a path to the rear of the pub, Howard following dutifully but less expertly behind; by the time he'd reached the door to the back bar, Malcolm had already vanished inside.

'Here, where do you think you're going?' came an angry high-pitched squeal as he made to push open the door. A short, fat balding queen in lilac shirt and henna rinse had turned from gossipping with a friend and was now holding out his hand to him, glaring with tiny suspicious eyes from behind a small table carefully positioned near the doorway. 'If you want to go in there it'll cost you 30p — it's cabaret night tonight.'

'Oh I'm sorry, I didn't know, ' mumbled Howard, reddening in embarrassment like a small child caught stealing, and hurriedly reaching in his pocket for more money.

'Oh *didn't* you? Well you do *now*, ' the doorman snapped, smiling scornfully at his friend and flinging Howard's coins contemptuously into a tin on the table beside him. His podgy, beringed fingers tore savagely at a little book of flimsy paper tickets, and he tossed one in Howard's direction, his puffy eyes screwing up in spiteful amusement as Howard was forced to stoop down to retrieve it from the floor.

The back bar was if anything more crowded than the front, and if its occupants had been attracted by the promise of a cabaret, they were sadly disappointed. The tiny stage at the far end was bare, save for a small electric organ with no one playing; and the only form of entertainment, if such it could be called, came from a worn-out juke-box in the corner. Nor did the prospective audience seem to be entertaining themselves very much; a few hardy souls were chatting and laughing in small groups, but the majority stood alone, pressed closely together in the semi-darkness like bedenimed sardines, silently drinking and eyeing each other with hopeful suspicion.

At first Howard had great difficulty in finding Malcolm; many times he thought he'd spotted his denim jacket and check shirt in the crowd, only to discover on closer inspection that they belonged to someone else. Eventually he located him leaning against the bar, and hurried over apologising for his absence; but if Malcolm had missed him in the intervening period, he didn't show it.

'Oh Howard, there you are,' he said regretfully, frowning down at him. He indicated a tall moustached man standing next to him, whom he had been chatting to when Howard approached. 'This is Tony. Tony, this is Howard, my flatmate.'

Tony's cold dark eyes surveyed Howard questioningly.

'Your flatmate?' he enquired cautiously.

'Yes, that's right,' said a sheepish Howard, blushing again, though he didn't know why.

'My previous flatmate moved out a few months ago, so I put an advert for the room in *Time Out* and Howard answered it,' explained Malcolm hastily, lest Tony should harbour any wrong impressions as to why he and Howard should be living together.

'Oh I see,' said Tony and saw fit to give Howard a wan smile.
'Through the accommodation ads in *Time Out*, eh? So you didn't
know each other before then?' he added, just to make sure.

'Oh no, not at all,' replied Malcolm, laughing gaily as if the very
idea that he should have known Howard for a long time was
ridiculous. 'Oh no, Howard was just looking for a place to live and
I happened to have a room in my flat going vacant, that's all. He
hasn't been living in London for very long. Still finding his way
about, aren't you? He's from up North,' Malcolm explained,
smiling significantly at Tony, who nodded back and smiled
commiseratingly at Howard.

They stood in a silent circle, glancing distractedly around the
room and wondering what to say next.

'Can I get you a drink?' asked Tony graciously, at length.

'Same again please,' said Malcolm, handing Tony his empty
glass.

'Oh thank you,' stammered Howard, to whom the question had
originally been asked. 'I'll have half a bitter, please.'

'Tony's the guy I mentioned before, you know, the one I saw in
the loo,' explained Malcolm in a low voice as Tony pushed his way
further down the bar to try and attract the barman's attention.
'He seems quite keen. We were having a nice little chat before you
arrived.'

There was another rather awkward pause until Tony brought
the drinks.

'Well, cheers,' said Tony, raising his glass.

They silently sipped their beer and Howard began to wish he
hadn't come. It wasn't as if he had ever wanted to in the first place.
It had been Malcolm's idea; that morning, as they had begun their
separate journeys together on the bus, Malcolm had suddenly
made the invitation, feeling the need for some sort of company
that evening and at that particular moment lacking any better
choice of partner. And now it seemed, having found a better one in
Tony, he wanted Howard to disappear just as quietly as he'd
assented to come along. But it would be rude to suddenly go off
and leave them after Tony had just bought him a drink, Howard
decided. He glanced anxiously around him, considering what to
do, wondering why he always allowed himself to be persuaded into
coming to these places when he knew he really didn't like them.
The mild excitement of anticipation as he waited outside the pub
plucking up courage to go in was unfortunately never satisfied by
the stark reality of the drab interior where the same old scene of
dull resignation and hopeful flickerings played out on the same

bored faces. Or so it seemed to him anyway; Malcolm usually managed to enjoy himself here. 'I think of this place as our local,' he was saying to Tony, trying to pretend that Howard wasn't there.' Even though it's quite a way away, it's the nearest gay pub to where we live.' Howard reminded himself that he was still very new to it all and there was still a great deal he didn't know. But he did wish he were better equipped to deal with these social situations.

He was saved from further embarrassment by the sudden termination of the juke-box and a flurry of activity around the stage which drew everyone's attention: it was rumoured that the promised cabaret had finally got itself together and was about to appear. Eventually from behind a tattered curtain strung rather ineffectually across one side of the stage there stepped a small round man wearing a dark brown toupee, a bright red jacket and a bow-tie. He stepped nimbly across the tiny stage to take his place at the organ, blowing kisses and waving to his friends in the audience, and began to play a medley of songs from assorted musicals, everyone hoped as a warm-up to some following main attraction.

'Oh this is very boring,' yawned Malcolm twenty minutes later when the man started playing *Don't Rain On My Parade* for the second time. 'Isn't anyone else on tonight besides Liberace here?'

'Does it matter? None of them are ever worth watching anyway,' replied Tony, who had purposefully kept his back to the stage and was staring at Malcolm instead, making desultory conversation and buying him drinks, a silly expectant grin across his face. He had a rather dog-like look, emphasised by hopeful dark brown eyes, drooping moustache and soft wet lips, thought Howard, put out by the way the other two kept ignoring him.

'But having paid for a cabaret I do expect one,' said Malcolm stubbornly, his voice rising clearly above the discontented murmur of the crowd around him. 'And where is it, I'd like to know? Surely they haven't got the cheek to call this one!' He glared accusingly at the organist who fortunately couldn't see him where he stood sulking at the bar.

'I don't really see why it should bother you so much,' said Tony, beginning to look rather bored.

'The cabaret's late as usual,' the barman informed them as he leant across to collect Malcolm's assortment of empty glasses. 'She always keeps us waiting on a Friday night if she can. Likes to spoil the start of the weekend, the miserable cow. There you are,' he went on, bringing Malcolm and Tony another drink. 'The fat old bag must have got herself ready at last — listen, he's playing her cue. And not before bloody time!' he shouted as the star of the evening appeared, but his words were lost amid the din of clapping, cheering and cat-calls that greeted her as she swept her way to the front of the stage. The reception also drowned out the announcement of her name by the man at the organ, so that Howard had no idea who it was he was clapping, though it really didn't matter.

She burst immediately into song, not bothering to stop and greet her friends as the organist had done — indeed, judging from the conversations Howard could hear around him, it didn't appear that she had many. Fortunately her loud and hoarse rendition of *There's Such a Lot of Living to Do* was sufficiently drowned by the energetic playing of the organist to make it tolerable, so that some people in the audience actually seemed to be enjoying the performance. Malcolm concentrated on Tony instead, chatting flirtatiously and throwing him what he hoped were mysterious and exciting smiles. Tony grinned back, like a besotted labrador; Howard ignored them both, finding the singer a more interesting object to study.

As the barman had remarked, she was undeniably fat, which was not exactly disguised by the tight pink satiny dress she had chosen to wear, its wide fish-tail skirt billowing out around her large stilettoed feet like yards of pink net curtaining. The strawberry-blond cottage loaf on her head didn't produce a very flattering effect, either; Howard found her whole appearance grotesque and overblown. But perhaps that was what she was trying to achieve; she was certainly like no woman of his own generation.

She finished singing just as Malcolm moved closer to Tony, and the prolonged if ironic round of applause which followed covered whatever words passed between them; but Howard was sure they were talking about him, which seemed confirmed a few minutes later when they both made their way to the back of the room. Howard didn't know why they felt the need to bother, considering they'd hardly said a word to him during the past half-hour. To make things even easier for them, and now quite glad to get away from their company, he pushed his way closer to the stage; the chanteuse was now standing at the very front of it, looking out over the crowded bar. Her dark eyes, hooded beneath their halos of false eyelashes, squinted out restlessly over the assembly, noting who was and who wasn't applauding and picking out individuals who might make useful scapegoats later on in her act, a fate which Malcolm and Tony had escaped by prudently retiring out of sight. She smiled cynically down at her audience.

'How are you sweethearts?' she called in mock concern. 'Have you missed your auntie Gertie?'

There followed a brief verbal battle in which Gertie and her audience exchanged a barrage of carefully rehearsed insults, and she then began to tell a long and complicated story about her misadventures with the chimney-sweep who had come to unblock her flue the other day. Malcolm, made careless by the drink, tittered a few times until he saw that Tony wasn't at all amused by Gertie's reminiscences; after that he kept a straight face and concentrated instead on his lager. But plenty of others in the audience seemed to find it funny, as even the worst jokes can be when you're bored and have got a few drinks inside you. Even though he too found himself laughing occasionally, Howard was hardly overimpressed by the act, and soon found himself glancing distractedly about the room in search of further recreation. Most of the people surrounding him, mainly male but with a smattering of women, were paying at least some degree of attention to the monologue; a notable exception being a lesbian couple drinking and chatting together by the bar, their backs deliberately turned away from the stage. Howard gave a slight smile as his eyes travelled over them; he admired them for their show of defiance at something that so clearly didn't interest them. A lot of the men gave the appearance of enjoying the cabaret, laughing and bitching together in small groups, or smiling to themselves from their solitary positions amongst the crowd. But not everyone was smiling; Howard's eyes were suddenly caught by a young man leaning against the wall in the corner, scowling back at the game being played out on the stage.

It was strange, he was not the usual sort of person to attract Howard, who would normally have steered well clear of the shock of white peroxide hair, the three glass earrings in the left ear, and the thick line of kohl across his eyes, which made them look like fierce black slits as he screwed up his face at the performer. But for some reason, perhaps boredom, or an oppressive sense of isolation, or, taking a cue from the lesbian couple whose laughter and chatter were getting noticeably louder in the background, perhaps just from plain contrariness — for whatever reason, he felt compelled to squeeze himself over towards the young man, whose aggressive stance ensured there was plenty of empty space nearby that Howard could make for.

Despite the uncomfortably blatant exterior (or perhaps because of it, Howard didn't know) the young man was really rather pretty; so Howard decided, as he studied the generous mouth and sensitive blue eyes that hid behind the angry expression. The young man suddenly caught him staring, and taken unawares, smiled back, dissolving his aggression into a wide and friendly grin that lit up his face and made Howard glad he had come along that evening after all. With rising confidence, he made his way through the smoke and bodies to where the young man was waiting.

'Hello,' said Howard rather awkwardly, but at least being bold for once.

'Hello,' said the young man, still smiling.

'I'm Howard. What's your name?' said Howard simply, trying to keep the conversation going, though at a loss for words. But that seemed to be enough. Smiling at Howard's openness, the young man replied, 'I'm Steve.' But before either of them could proceed from here, they were startled by an outraged shriek from the stage.

For one fearful moment, Howard thought that he and Steve were to be the butt of the artiste's fury, for having dared to speak while her act was still in progress; then he realised that the target was to be the two lesbians by the bar, whose conversation was beginning to drown out some of the throwaway lines, hard enough to appreciate at the best of times. She stood poised like a painted harpy at the edge of the stage, her lips open in an angry leer, revealing large and expensive white teeth and a fat pink tongue whose soft wet appearance belied its sharpness. Her dark eyes flashed with unsuppressed malice.

'I don't mind you keeping your backs to me because it's a fucking sight better than having to see your faces, but I don't want to hear your bleeding voices booming out all through my act,' she sneered contemptuously across the room, buoyed up by the wave of laughter greeting this remark that came from some of the men in the audience.

One of the lesbians turned to look back with equal contempt, her eyes pinning the performer with studied indifference. 'Why on earth should we listen to a ridiculous old queen like you?' she said in a loud but controlled voice that rang clearly across the suddenly silent room, and went back to talking animatedly with her friend.

'Why don't you piss off, you old wanker?' came a sudden shout at Howard's side. He turned to see Steve glaring up at the stage, and was immediately acutely embarrassed; but at the same time he was unable to look away from a scene which gripped him with a savage fascination.

These two latter remarks brought more laughter from the rest of the assembly, but of a kind quite unwelcome to the injured artiste. Her dark eyes blazing beneath their fringes of mascara, the red gloss of her lips set into a grim and vengeful smile, she drew herself up to her full seven feet, with the help of the high wig and five-inch stilettos that groaned and teetered beneath her massive bulk. Her imposing stance caused an impressed hush to fall over the audience; she made use of the pause to choose the right words to demolish her opponents.

'Listen, you apology for a woman,' she began, but was allowed to go no further.

'Who the hell do you think you're talking to mate?' came the angry shout of the other lesbian, who became the new focus of attention as she advanced towards the stage, her friend close behind, cutting a path through the crowd of gay men like a hot knife through butter. The barman, who had been listening to the interchange with evident enjoyment, suddenly began to look anxious.

'You could never hope to be a millionth as much of a woman as she is, you faded old drag-queen,' Steve taunted, casting appealing glances at Howard for support. Howard was forced to respond, feeling unable to walk away and pretend nothing had happened, for once involved in the rights and wrongs of the situation. He found himself nodding in agreement, standing even closer to Steve to demonstrate his open solidarity. On the edges of the crowd he saw Malcolm staring out at him in shocked disbelief.

'Do we really have to put up with this shit any longer?' Steve demanded, turning back to the rest of the audience, emboldened by Howard's support. 'Why should we pay money for the privilege of being ripped off and insulted?'

At this point the barman, deciding that enough questions had been asked for one night, called for reinforcements and came out from behind the bar.

'Alright, alright, that's enough,' he said authoritatively, indicating Steve and Howard. 'Gertie, get off the stage. The cabaret's over for tonight.'

This announcement drew cheers from some parts of the audience, which only rubbed the salt in Gertie's wounds. 'I'm certainly not going to get off when my act is only half-over,' he said indignantly, towering down from his position on the stage.

'Yes you bloody are!' shouted the two lesbians, who seemed to have won the support of a few more men and were making menacing gestures in front of the electric organ — the organist having deserted in alarm.

'Get him off! Get him off!' called Steve, with Howard feeling compelled to join in.

'Right you two,' said the barman, deciding that perhaps Howard and Steve would be the easier to tackle — 'Outside!Come on, get out the pair of you,' and began to push them towards the door. There was the expected scuffle as Steve resisted; he was soon locked in a struggle with the bar staff.

'Malcolm, come and help!' cried Howard, trying to come between Steve and the barman. 'Malcolm, please!'

Everyone's eyes suddenly turned to Malcolm who stood hesitant and embarrassed in the crowd, furious with Howard for making him such an unflattering centre of attention. Beside him Tony suddenly looked quite unwell; he sniffed self-consciously and glared his disapproval. 'If that's the sort of people you live with, you can forget it,' he said in a loud and injured tone, and stormed out through the front bar, leaving a rejected and indignant Malcolm behind him.

'Look what you've bloody well done now!' he screamed at Howard, waving his umbrella threateningly.

'Now then, that's enough,' said the barman; but as he spoke there was an anguished shriek. All eyes turned again to the stage; someone had climbed up and pulled off the drag artiste's wig. He stood unmasked in the spotlight, his pink and balding head shining ludicrously above his thick coating of white panstick, now beginning to run and smear as beads of sweat and tears of rage channelled their way down his fat shaking cheeks and over his powdered chest, to disappear in damp confusion down his artificial cleavage. That was the last impression Howard caught of him, while being hustled out of the pub by the barman and a couple of assistants.

'Get out and stay out!' shouted the barman as the three of them were thrown unceremoniously out on the street.

'How dare you throw me out like this? I've done nothing wrong!' retorted Malcolm aggrieved and affronted by what he saw as unfair treatment. 'I've a good mind to report you to the police.'

'You're bloody lucky I didn't call the police in tonight to charge you with using that umbrella as an offensive weapon. They'd 've soon sorted you out, don't worry. Why on earth did you lot have to cause trouble? You people are usually quiet, don't make any fuss, no heavy drunks and no punch-ups, that's why we like you as customers. Now look what you've done. You've only spoilt things for the others. Don't let me see any of you in here again.'

'Don't worry, none of us would dream of coming to your filthy exploitative pub again,' began Steve, his hands stuck defiantly in the pockets of his donkey-jacket; but before he could continue he was interrupted by Malcolm who cut in peevishly with 'I don't want to spoil things, I'm not like this lout. I've done nothing wrong, I'm innocent!' only to be answered by a burst of sarcastic laughter from within and the door slammed in his face.

'Well I for one shall never set my feet over the threshold of that place again,' said Malcolm, striding away from the pub and gripping the handle of his umbrella forcefully. 'And don't think Blondie here is going to set his feet over our doorstep either,' he hissed in Howard's ear. 'I'm not having him back in my flat, I warn you, not after tonight's little escapade. What on earth do you think you're doing, going with some weirdo like him? You ought to be ashamed of yourself, the way you made me a laughing stock in front of all my friends. I'll never be able to show my face in that pub again!'

'You just said you didn't want to, and anyway you've been barred by the management,' said Howard with deflating common sense, his mind strangely sharpened by the events of the evening. He smiled across at Steve, who stood encouragingly beside him, his white blond hair pleasantly dishevelled by his tussle in the pub, his blue eyes twinkling inside their vivid black stripes. Steve grinned back, sharing the same sense of exhilaration. 'You needn't get your knickers in a twist, Howard's coming back with me, aren't you Howard?' he said.

But though this news came as a welcome relief to Malcolm, it still meant the three of them had to share a bus ride, as it turned out Steve lived in the same direction, though in a far less salubrious suburb. No doubt in some dreadful squat, thought Malcolm, thinking with vindictive satisfaction of the cold and squalor Howard would be going back to. Still, judging by the state of Howard's bedroom, he'd probably feel quite at home there, and perhaps on reflection it was where he belonged. Malcolm certainly didn't feel able to live with him any longer, not after what had happened that night and the way Howard had let him down. And when he'd done him the favour of inviting him out for a drink; he cursed Howard's lack of gratitude and was glad he had finally seen through all his games. Let him go off to a filthy squat with this punk hooligan; he could go and move in there for all Malcolm cared. When he next got him alone without his delinquent companion, he would tell him flat to take his belongings and good riddance. He doubted if Howard would adapt very well to the discomforts of squatting, though he suspected that once Howard started to slide, he might prove capable of anything. Look at the way he was sitting opposite and laughing unconcernedly with that awful Steve, completely unbothered by the obvious fact that he had .ruined Malcolm's evening.

Malcolm was relieved when the two of them rose to take their leave; he was further delighted to see that it was raining again and they would be sure to get soaked. He held tightly on to his umbrella and ignored their departure, not bothering to say goodbye but looking instead at his reflection in the window, thrown back at him by the black and cloudy night outside. He patted his hair carefully back into place, reasserting his image, and saw with annoyance that the rain had already slackened. Glancing back as the bus drew away, he caught sight of the two of them walking shameless and brazen with their arms round each other, laughing their way down the road together. It had been a terrible evening, Malcolm decided, still agitated as he stumbled to his feet a few minutes later to get off at his stop. Thank goodness he had got Howard off his hands for the night, and hopefully would soon have him off his hands forever; he could now go back to the flat alone and escape the world and its pressures.

This pleasing thought gave Malcolm some comfort, and he stepped off the bus with a certain grim satisfaction, ignoring the oppressive black clouds still gathered overhead. Only with the first heavy drops of a new downpour did he realise that he'd left his umbrella on the bus, which was now out of sight round the corner.

extract from
ELEMENTS OF A COFFEE SERVICE

by Robert Glück

One morning I was walking Lily around 28th and Sanchez. Lily, whose motto is better safe than sorry, trotted not too far ahead, avoiding Dobermans and saying hello to pedestrians, gravely accepting their compliments — her gold eyelashes and extravagant tail. A Chevy pick-up turned the corner in front of me and I probably looked too hard at the man in the passenger seat, who had a profile, because all at once they started yelling faggot and fucking faggot. I had been in a happy mood and with the last of my ebullience I gave them the finger, which I instantly regretted because the truck screeched to a stop and lurched into a three-point turn. There were four, they were laughing and yelling. Lily and I took off. We ran down Sanchez and turned back down the corner on 29th along with the truck. One of them missed me with a beer can. They were laughing and driving parallel with us, but then we cut across 29th, leapt up a retaining wall and through a cyclone fence by way of a hole I knew about. The fence surrounded a large field where I sometimes walk Lily late at night, giving her an opportunity to roam around a little on her own and to enjoy some damp plant and earth smells.

If they didn't separate the advantage was mine because the field had entrances at both sides. I stood in the centre on cut grass in broad daylight, expensive suburban daylight; two blocks away bells began swinging towards noon, and they wouldn't attack someone in broad daylight unless of course they would. You'll understand my fear because television trained us to understand the fear of a running man. I hoped for no police cars because attacking a homosexual is not such a clear-cut offence as, say, stealing a package of processed cheese. The odour of cut grass reminded me of my mother's childhood in Denver because she always says it reminds her of that. She lived there during the summers with my great-aunt Charlotte, a regal woman who fed

the children tubs of strawberries in heavy cream and bakery bread
with huge slabs of butter. That was before the days of cholesterol.
But Charlotte advocated health foods, brown rice and no sugar,
which took some independence fifty years ago. She had plenty to
spare. I remember after Uncle Harry's funeral the doorbell rang
and an immense basket of fruit from Denver was delivered into my
mother's hands. The delivery man said very soberly, 'Mrs Isaacs
wanted to be especially sure you received this message from her.
Wash it before you eat it.' Then I recalled my mother's recent
phone conversation with Charlotte who said, 'You were such a
pretty girl, are you still pretty?' And my mother replied,
'Charlotte, I'm pushing sixty.' My mother, who is first and
foremost a grand-daughter, a daughter, sister, cousin, niece, wife,
mother, sister-in-law, aunt and grandmother. So far the incident
was nothing much and it had happened fast but it bore the
sluggishness that precedes violence. So I tried to reassure myself
with the safety of family memories of childhoods and old ages.

On the other hand, I had ample time to remember Kevin's
bashed-in teeth, Bruce getting rousted and then rousted again by
the police, and the time one Halloween when a man yelling queer
charged Ed and me with a metal pipe; and recall an acquaintance,
hardly a face even, who one day sat on the blue chenille of the
couch in my kitchen. He was murdered by someone he brought
home, the neighbours saw the killer's face on and off during the
night. That's the logical conclusion to this catalogue of betrayals,
the murderer takes you when you're naked and expect tenderness
and each by agreement is the host to the other's vulnerability. The
sky clouded over allowing the green, which had been over-
exposed, to relax into its full colour. Recalling these events did
not necessarily indicate great extremity, they are not isolated in
the way the grammar of sentence and paragraph isolate them. The
threat of physical violence makes one part of the whole. College
and my literary education agreed that I should see myself as a
random conjunction of life's possibilities, certainly an enviable,
luxurious point of view. But it's hard to draw on that as a model
when four men are chasing you down the street. The problem cuts
both ways. What life will that model sustain, and when aren't we
being chased? The truck circled, pulled over at the entrance on
30th, the men piled out. I waited until they were out of the truck,
then exited at the opposite side with Lily keeping close to my legs.
She was vibrant and totally into the escape. We ran around the
block and slipped into a produce market.

The store was filled with strawberries and the odour of

strawberries. I picked two baskets, making sure that they were red
on the bottom as well as on top, that they weren't mouldy, that
they smelled strong and healthy. People from Thailand ran the
store, and oddly, it seemed to me, they had the country-western
music station playing. 'Stand by Your Man' by Tammy Wynette,
Willie Nelson's intimate version of 'Georgia On My Mind' —
intelligent song, and the Eagles' song that begins by drawing out
the beautiful word 'desperado'. Then there was the kind of song I
like a lot, where two people exchange verses answering and
explaining. He worked on the dayshift and her husband worked
on the nightshift. They lived in Pittsburgh and you could call
them the Pittsburgh Steelers because, in voices resonant with
country-western pain that made the joke dimensional, they stole
love and pleasure whenever they got the chance. You might think
that I like the song because I identify but that would be wrong.
Their love was a child's secret hiding-place for chocolate, hidden
in the difference between their needs and their lives. It's true that I
carry in my spine, wrists and knees the glance of a man I passed
three years ago walking up 18th Street, and the shock I felt on
seeing that he was completely to my taste. But the difference
between these plaintive singers and myself is greater. The
difference: one night walking down Westwood a bunch of people
in a car yelled faggot at me.

The song ended and then I heard the sound of brakes screeching
and then one, two, three, thud! somebody's in trouble. We looked
through the window to see the pick-up piled into a telephone pole.
A fender was balled up like tin foil and they stood there wearing
uncertain smiles, looking small and bewildered. I picked out the
attractive one and when he turned I saw he was holding his hands
in front of a mess of blood on his face. I stood a minute, enjoying
the sheer pleasure of breathing in and out. I resolved to make my
bed, throw away papers, read Gramsci's *Prison Notebooks*, have an
active — no, a famous social life.

Of course that makes for a satisfying if frivolous ending. What
really happened was that the men and the truck disappeared
except from my imagination. I had angry dreams. Even in my
erotic fantasies I couldn't banish a violence that twisted the plot
away from pleasure to confusion and fear. And what I resolved was
this: that I would gear my writing to tell you about incidents like
the one at 29th and Church, to put them to you as real questions
that need answers, and that these questions, along with my
understanding and my practice, would grow more energetic and
precise.

TROUT DAY (by pumpkin-light)

by Adam Mars-Jones

Jim hardly sees the black and orange streamers which decorate the lobby for the Costume Ball, or the dish of pumpkin-seeds laid out in welcome on the table there.

There are three light-sources in the room he is approaching. Behind the beer-table at far left stands a traditional jack-o-lantern, carved and prepared by the Education Officer, who is now a purple dragon with only a beard and a paper cup showing beneath its papier-mâché snout.

The Dragon-Officer scorns the low-caste pumpkins sold in town, piled outside the supermarkets like misshapen beach-balls. Every year he drives out into the country and prowls around pumpkin-patches till he finds his phrenological ideal, every bump and lobe perfectly defined.

Back home he observes the simple rules of the operation:

1. Make sure you cut an irregular lid so you can see right away which way it goes back on.

2. Hold the knife at a shallow angle when you cut the lid so it can't drop thru.

3. Carve the features on the bevel to help the light spread out.

The resulting jack-o-lantern is almost Apollonian, in spite of the carefully-etched scar and the thread of pumpkin-pulp dangling from the edge of its mouth. The mild golden light and the high pondering forehead make it a downright reassuring bogy.

So too the ferocity of its maker's dragon-outfit is compromised by the soulful eyelash-fringes he has given it.

Placed at center left of the back wall is a dayglo midget of orange plastic, with a pumpkin instead of a head and a top hat perched above it, politely half-raised. He is lit up from inside and throws a miserly ellipse of orange-red against the wall.

Given pride of place on top of the tv is a second authentic jack-o-lantern, but this one's face is a crude piece of work, suggesting idiocy not menace. Mounted inside it, wedged into the flesh, is a strobe-light which gives off a bone-white flash several times a second; a lightning to match the thunder of the sound-system.

The scooped-out skull, with its out-sticking pieces of metal and wire, looks like propaganda against electroshock therapy, so a sun-hat has been used to conceal them.

Stroboscopes have been known to trigger off *petit mal* attacks, even in subjects with no history of epilepsy; the stuttering flashes interfere with the brain's own dance-rhythms. So the organizers of this event have instructions to look out for any jerks and seizures which go beyond permissible disco. No one pretends this will be easy.

Jim hardly sees the black and orange streamers which decorate the lobby for the Costume Ball, or the bowl of pumpkin-seeds laid out in welcome on the table there.

Pumpkin-seeds make a popular and tasty party snack; just soak a few hours in salted water, then dry off in the oven. The seeds Jim has been eating are less traditional, though by the standards of his friends they mark him as an anachronism.

When planted in the normal way, the earth's metabolism turns them duly into plants; but in the human body they act as mild psychotropics. They 'alter consciousness'. They screen an hour or two of eyelid movies. They rubberize a few perceptual grids.

The U.S. Government dislikes these effects, and arranges for the seeds to be sprayed with a preparation which multiplies their slight natural toxicity. They are then rejected by birds and bugs, and by the digestive systems of thrill-seekers.

Jim's source, though, has promised him a purity of one hundred per cent.

Jim makes final adjustments to his head-dress. His handsome features, including green stupid eyes and a dark-blond mustache, are dimly visible through the coarse mesh of a veil which suggests both a vamp and a bee-keeper.

He is as old as sin, if sin is twenty-six.

Arriving at the desk, Jim pays the entrance fee and receives on his wrist a purple lambda in Magic Marker, which will qualify him for re-admission if he leaves and comes back. Lambda is the symbol of international gay liberation. T-shirts with a mock-fraternity logo, tri-Lambda, are currently in preparation.

The faint-hearted opt for a more abstract wrist-mark, since the dye takes some days to wash out.

Here at the desk Jim receives the first of many routine compliments on his costume. He wears a pale-green jump suit, its sleeves short, a large cornflower embroidered down one leg.

His slightly convex stomach looms a little through the fabric, confident like Snoopy's of being liked for itself. Rustling wings are formed along his arms by wide feathers of tissue paper, in shades of green. An effect of ethereal vigor   is achieved.

Once inside the Informal Lounge, Jim weaves his way across to the beer keg, though several drinks are already contributing to the impure flux inside him. The music IT'S FUN TO STAY AT THE YMCA drowns out extended conversation, but there is much nodding and smiling.

A passing GI asks whether he is Oberon or Titania. Jim shakes his head and leans across to shout 'FELLINI-SATYRICON', through his veil, into the military ear.

Maybe two dozen people are dancing. Twice as many watch them, or pretend to watch while jockeying for position or edging up to each other. The secret is not to expect a welcome. Instead you should materialize just inside your target's peripheral vision as a rampant sex-object. Moments ago you were furniture, now you are sheer tantalizing Other. Keep saying this to yourself.

More people are arriving all the while.

The tape fades out 'YMCA' and starts on 'Fire Island'. A ripple of pleasure passes across the floor. This song has won many fans with its cheery out-chorus of Don't Go In The Bushes.

Mighty Mouse, a correction officer from Harrisonburg, is the first to ask Jim for a dance. His costume — cape, T-shirt and shorts; running shoes and superhero tights — is designed to turn his littleness to good effect. Mighty Mouse asks all his acquaintances in turn for one dance, coaxes wallflowers out onto the floor, speaks well of everyone. He respects the Personal Space of those around him, which greatly surprises them in this context.

The community reels from his reckless goodmouthing.

There are several styles of dancing already competing on the floor. Dwayne, wearing the Dancing Queen T-shirt he premiered at last year's Marathon, leads a line of followers through an intricate routine. He is as grim as a commando barking telepathic orders, and resentful of anyone who gets in the way of maneuvers.

The guys with the wild elbow-language, doing the splits and high-kicks, watched *Soul Train* this afternoon. They are hoping that natural-sense-of-rhythm will turn out to be their birthright too.

A hard-hat and a cowboy are ignoring each other at point-blank range. In butch dancing of this type the priorities are strutting and stamping. The music's rhythm becomes something to be resisted and brought to heel. To surrender would be as bad as failing a chromosome test. Feet turned out, these masterful slobs rebut, second-by-second, the world's accusations of exquisiteness.

Established couples step and spin with practised smoothness. Issues of leading and following are settled by tiny signals, eye-sent and eye-caught, and tiny pressures of hand on waist or hand.

Unaccustomed pairs, like Jim and Mouse, bob and stride in each other's direction, free-style.

Jim's eyes close as he dances, and his lips shape themselves into a gruff pout. He appreciates his steps ungrudgingly.

Punk-rocker dances with Dracula, dragon with convict, Tin Man with Straw Man. Cowardly Lion has presumably backed out at the last moment, and will not find his Courage tonight.

Inexperienced and poorly coordinated, Mighty Mouse moves his feet but not his body, as others on the floor immobilize their hips or arms or shoulders. He watches Jim, who is now showing the ceiling a clenched fist, all the time they are dancing.

The GI is now dancing with an enigma in black tie and gorilla-mask. No one knows who it is under the costume, only that it must be hell in there. Someone may be curious enough to go home with him.

When the song ends, Jim says 'Wonderful' and Mighty Mouse thanks him. Jim returns to the beer-table.

Mighty Mouse looks around him. The eyes beneath his ebbing hair-line are radiant with fun-hunger, but when he stays behind each week to help clear up he seems perfectly content to be escorting no more than a broom.

Maybe drinking a few beers satisfies the animalistic outsider in him; for of course in Virginia, the statutes of the Alcoholic Beverages Commission prohibit the supply of alcohol to homo-sexuals. A little liquid wrongdoing may amount (in the mind of a correction officer) to a potent flirtation with his pariah status.

Notice the similarity to the Wild West, where the White Man (speaking-with-forked-tongue) kept the Red Man well away from the fatal fire-water. And the history of the Indian offers a cheering precedent. Survivors of purges can become wonderfully fashionable.

A glistening Indian, fresh from tangoing with a sheik, nods to Mighty Mouse's smile and is asked to dance.

As Jim refills his cup from the keg, he notices a youth with a beautiful uninhabited profile standing awkwardly by the soft-drink cooler. He wears a Jacobethan doublet and hose. If this stranger hopes to stay within the law as a teetotaller he is deluded. ABC statutes in any case forbid the serving of alcohol in a place where homosexuals 'congregate' (to plan their color-schemes, hen-parties, orphanage-raids).

Jim smiles and gets going on a little small-talk: 'What's your costume?'

'Uh . . . Formal Faggot I guess.' The boy smiles back. 'Hamlet in Act Two. You?'

'Fellini-Satyricon.' Jim's genital brain tells him a little more charm is called for.

This will be his last wholly conscious move of the evening.

'Reel Three', he says. 'Like to dance?'

Jim's dancing is much more purposeful now that it is a matter of erotic reflex. His strategy is to follow, but aggressively; molding himself to his partner's steps, but forcing him backwards.

Hamlet is easily wrongfooted. When his steps are brought to his attention in this way, he remembers he has no idea what he is doing. In self-defensive embarrassment he raises his hands to Jim's shoulders. Soon they are dancing close.

Jim's romantic involvements last three days on average. He blames biorhythms.

A premature slow-dance follows the fast one on the tape. Jim grips Hamlet firmly and sways to the new tempo.

> ONCE WE WERE LOVERS
> CAN'T THEY UNDERSTAND
> CLOSER THAN OTHERS I WAS YOUR
> I WAS YOUR MAN

Without a deejay to bully them into cooling it down whether they want to or not, the masqueraders at first hold back from the floor. Then figures from the edges of the room move in for a provisional kill.

Their smiles are a little more authentic than the letters pages of magazines they hide at home.

> DON'T TALK OF HEARTACHES
> I REMEMBER THEM ALL
> AND I'M — CHECKING YOU OUT ONE
> NIGHT
> TO SEE — IF I'M FAKING IT ALL

Jim murmurs incoherently in Hamlet's ear through the beer-sticky webbing, listing and exploring the hiding-places of cuteness.

There is a species of mantis whose female bites off her husband's head during early foreplay, leaving him to administer the conjugals on Automatic Pilot.

She has sound evolutionary reasons for this, but her lover can't hear them. He continues to go through the motions, and here among the higher primates, so does Jim.

> SO MANY OTHERS
> SO MANY TIMES
> SIXTY NEW CITIES AND WHAT DO I —
> WHAT DO I FIND?

As the dance goes on, more and more of Jim's weight is transferred to Hamlet's shoulders. By its end, Jim's knees are near the floor and Hamlet is barely able to move.

Devotees of the Latin Hustle have by now tracked beer across the floor in sticky swirls and arabesques. It is like dancing on flypaper. Torn-down streamers of orange and black get wet and bleed their dye. Broad fronds of green tissue from Jim's molting wings are trampled, down among the cigarette-butts.

In his desperation Hamlet catches the attention of a tall man standing nearby, who carries a fan and wears a kimono.

Hand-painted characters adorn the panels of the fan and also his ethnic undergarment, not now on show. On his feet are the traditional wooden sandals, thick rectangles supported by four blunt wooden pegs; they look like little coffee-tables.

Between them Hamlet and the stranger get Jim to a chair, and then the Kimono-Man brings him a cup of water. After a couple of sips he says, 'Bathroom.'

Jim is supported along the corridor to the men's room. He pulls up his veil and is immediately, effortlessly sick into the consoling bowl.

His escorts leave him propped up against a stall, taking it easy behind closed lids.

In these special circumstances the men's room is a DMZ. The fluorescent strips over the mirrors are no competition for the flash and glow of pumpkin-light harsh and considerate. No one would cruise here by preference.

The players come here to take time out from the game. Only a merrymaker left over from the Trout Day banquet down the hall, flushed with fine wine and the excitement of the tackle auction, makes eye-contact of any kind; and looks down at his feet for the rest of his visit.

Here away from the music, a little pure conversation is carried on. A sweet-faced Pierrot with a disconcerting crimson codpiece removes his make-up and murmurs 'Zit City next stop' to the mirror.

Two of the Andrews Sisters practise their crosstalk.

'All *David* wants is a husband.'

'Don't you believe it. He'll settle for two legs and a pulse.'

'Now isn't that the pot calling the kettle beige?'

But drag is wildly unpopular here in the late late-seventies, and the Sisters will have to work hard to get laughs.

Forbidden minorities develop their own exclusion-principles. They catch on fast.

Jim gets up off the ground and washes his face.

As he wanders along the corridor back to the Lounge, his way is blocked by a small group of people. Two blacks are interrogating a piratical figure who wears a delicate mask of feathers. This is Mother.

Mother is a veteran and a long-time spokesman for the group. He belongs to the Old Guard of zapping. This confrontation is kid-stuff for him.

Jim leans against the wall to give moral support.

'Thar women in thar?' asks one of the blacks.

'Gay women, yes,' Mother tells him.

'See what I mean,' he says to his friend.

Mother is used to more abrasive encounters. His latest suggestion for the group, roundly defeated when it came to a vote, involved a poster, to read: HEY STRAIGHT WORLD! HOMOSEXUALS IN CHARLOTTESVILLE GAVE X (figure preferably in millions) PINTS OF BLOOD LAST MONTH. DON'T YOU OWE IT TO YOUR LOVED ONES TO DILUTE THIS FILTH BEFORE IT 'SAVES A LIFE'? The other members are happier Earning The Goodwill Of The Community.

The second intruder tries his hand.

'Thar women in thar?' he asks.

'Gay women, yes,' Mother tells him.

'See what I mean,' his friend says.

Mother outstares the two of them without any trouble. It is a small triumph now that the great days of zapping are over.

Mother affects a truckeresque beer-gut which is hopelessly out of date. He is anachronistic enough to enjoy dope even now, and to own the big bike his style of dress suggests.

Exponents of Zapping-à-la-mode are much too cosmopolitan to stay in town for this dance; they are up in D.C. on the weekend, where they can find the international set and a wide range of 3-D movies. Nouveau Zapping goes to a gym, keeps its hair and beard trimmed, and buys those tough hardwearin' clothes from specialty stores (Chez Gomorrah, The Dude Ranch) advertized in the Washington *Blade.*

Blocking the pass, the Old Guard relives old victories; days when Society was brought up short. Face to face with its contradictions.

Shocked into a new awareness.

Days when the world stirred in its sleep. Days when men were men, and the future was pure Frontier.

Mother lays down the law. 'The women here don't go for what you've got,' he says with showdown flatness. The two blacks retreat to the end of the corridor.

'Nothing personal you understand,' Mother calls after them as he and Jim return to the music and the beer-table.

On the way they pass two Fat Schoolboys with Measles sitting nervously near the desk. These two have come here, where the wild things are, to get themselves an authentic frisson. A jack-o - lantern no longer gives them chills, so they have chosen a more advanced bogy. Right now they are too scared to go in any further.

They have greatly overestimated the candlepower of deviance. But if they are lucky a swaying hairdresser will accost them.

Back in the half-dark, Mother pats most of the bodies he passes. Old Zapping spreads itself just as thin as New, thin as fallout or gold-leaf.

Almost everyone is dancing now, responding to the plaintive aggression of the current anthem.

Mighty Mouse dances with Anonymous Gorilla, Straw Man with Tin Man, Hamlet with Gertrude Stein of all people. The Kimono-Man dances with Dracula, flinging his clogs about like a berserk geisha.

(I gotta be a) MACHO MACHO MAN
(I gotta be a) MUCHO MACHO MAN

The vocal group performing this piece was recruited by an advert in the San Francisco *Advocate.* The wording stressed looks (Hot Hunks Wanted); singing voices (No Mutes Need Apply) were not a priority. That's the rumor anyway.

I AM (I AM)
WHAT I AM (WHAT I AM)
WHAT I AM — I'LL BE

You could filter out the music and concentrate on the complex soundtrack left behind. Synchronized handclaps and finger-popping on the beats;

regular stamping of feet, the Kimono-Man's wild clog-clatter above all;

the raucous sniff of a nose flooding its tissues with fun, from a bottle marked Liquid Aroma;

the tearing sound of soles pulled from a sticky floor;

and a communal whisper of wish-fulfilment as the crowd sings softly along.

I DID NOT CHOOSE THE WAY I AM
(but) I AM WHAT I AM . . .

After a long fade-out the last dance is announced. Jim makes his way over to where Hamlet is standing. Hamlet shrugs, and they dance.

Soon poor Donna Summer is in the grip of an asthmatic orgasm on the tape. Couples rotate unsteadily, or lean against each other like tent-poles. Many of the dancers continue to drink over their partners' shoulders. Mighty Mouse slow-dances with La Verne Andrews, Tin Man with Straw Man, Gertrude Stein with Isadora, Patti Andrews with Maxene Andrews.

Again Hamlet seeks out the Kimono-Man for help with Jim. When they get back to him, he is sitting on the floor and can only gasp 'Difficulty breathing'.

In this crisis the Kimono-Man is suddenly Hemingway. Telling Hamlet not to worry, he staggers with Jim out of the Lounge, into the cold air and across to his little Japanese auto.

They are only a few minutes away from the Hospital by car.

On the way Jim starts muttering something about kidneys. The Kimono-Man steps grimly on the gas.

He jumps several sets of lights in his hurry.

Then he realizes what Jim is saying. Jim is searching weakly through his costume, the words are 'kidney donor card', and he is doing his best to distribute his body after death as extravagantly as he has been doing in his life.

Jim falls silent for a few moments, but his breathing is easier. The Kimono-Man returns to obeying traffic-lights. Then Jim starts to speak again.

'If anything happens to me . . . ' he says ' . . . tell my friends . . . my good friends at Unitarian Church . . . ' At this point he falls silent again, and is snoring by the time they reach the hospital.

Nobody in the Emergency Room is surprised by the arrival of a towering Oriental supporting a bedraggled sprite. At Halloween, everything is weird so nothing is weird. Why else would it be the major gay festival? This October is National Hobbies Month; November will be devoted to Mental Retardation. Poised between them is a mildly distracting, mildly deranged celebration; one in which the family has little or no stake. Strangeness goes briefly unnoticed and unresented.

Jim is detained overnight as a precaution. The man in the kimono returns to the Informal Lounge to help clear up.

The mess is astounding. Mighty Mouse, working wonders with a broom, sums up the feeling of the helpers. For a bunch of supposed interior-decorators, we do great demolition.

Next day, Jim is discharged from hospital in good time to round up some friends for an almighty brunch. They put themselves outside huge platefuls of Steak'n'Eggs. They have themselves more than a few beers. Because people are wonderful. And when it's people you want, nothing else will do.

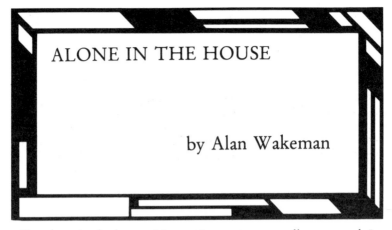

ALONE IN THE HOUSE

by Alan Wakeman

I'm alone in the house. Mummy's gone out to collect a parcel. I dont know what it is because she wouldnt tell me. But it must be something special and awful because she had her frightened look again. She said that when she comes back she doesnt want to find me here. She said I must go out and play with my friends and not come back till dark. She said she had a special reason for asking me to do this today and that one day I would understand. But I like it when I'm alone in the house. So I'm not going to go out. When she comes back, I'll run out the back door, and she wont know.

I'm in her bedroom. It smells of her in here. There are all sort of things she uses on her face and body. I wish mummy was happy. I wish I knew how to make her happy. There are all sorts of little bottles and jars on her dressingtable. I'm going to try them. I'm going to try what it feels like to be mummy. Even if I am a boy. Mummy says I cant use them because I'm a boy. But I dont care. I've watched her putting this stuff on her face. First she wipes it all with cotton wool, soaked in stuff from this bottle — like this. Then she puts some of this pink ointment on. Then rouge — like this. Now I dont look pale. Mummy's always saying how pale I look. Then she puts this pink powder over everything. Then, last of all, she puts lipstick on. I cant do it very well, but it doesnt really matter because mummy sometimes misses the shape of her lips too. Then she says: 'Oh, what the hell! Who's going to notice *me* anyway?' Once, I asked her why she puts all this stuff on, but she said it was too difficult to explain, and that I was too young to understand.

Now I know what it feels like to be mummy. I'm hiding behind all the smells and stuff. It feels very sad. I wouldnt want to play this game every day. But she does. She plays it every day. She doesnt play any other games at all. Once I asked her why she wears high-heeled shoes, because they make her trip up all the time, and she said that they made her legs look nice. I dont think mummy likes her *real* body.

Now I'm going to walk about the house and pretend that I'm mummy, doing the housework. Dusting, polishing, washing, hoovering, doing the washing up. 'Oh dear! Dirt everywhere. This needs cleaning. That needs cleaning. Never a moment's rest. I'm not cut out for this. I wanted to be a photographer and take beautiful photographs and have them printed in books, and be rich. And buy lots of nice clothes and go to Abroad. . .' (Abroad is a place mummy wants to go to, and she says if it wasnt for me and daddy, she could. . .) 'But no! Instead of going to Abroad, I'm alone in this bloody house, day after day, week after week, month after month, year after year. . . Alone in this bloody house!'

Now I'm in the front room. I'm pretending to clean the desk. There are lots of old photographs and letters. The photographs are from the time when mummy was at school, learning how to be a photographer. The letters are mostly from that time too. Most of them are from people I dont know, mummy says. People mummy knew in the old days 'before I was born'. Mummy was happy in the old days. When she talks about the friends she had then, her face looks different. One bundle of letters is from a special friend from the old days. Mummy says she was special because she loved mummy a lot. The letters frighten me a bit. They feel dangerous. Perhaps it's because they are from 'before I was born'. It frightens me to think of that time. No one will tell me where I was 'before I was born'. They just say 'heaven' if I try really hard to get an answer. But then they wont tell me where 'heaven' is. Mummy once said it was up in the sky. But I could tell she didnt really believe it. So I dont think she knows really. Although, sometimes, when she's very unhappy, she says she's going to go there, and then we'll all be sorry.

I keep telling mummy that daddy and I both love her very much, but I dont think she believes me. But if she does go to heaven one day, then she'll be happy. I know, because I've been there. I mean, I'm not *really* sure, but I think so. I think it's that place I can sometimes go to when I shut my eyes. I dont mean when I'm asleep. I mean when I'm alone in my room and sit on my bed, and shut my eyes, I can sometimes go to this secret place. I float up into the air and I can see my body, a long way away, down there, in my room. And then the beautiful colours come, and everything starts to be very exciting. And this beautiful young man comes and he takes my hand. His name is . . . Oh, I've just remembered, I'm not supposed to tell anyone his name. He said it's a secret between him and me. Anyway, he's very pretty. He has blue eyes and a black beard and curly blonde hair. He's the most beautiful person I've ever seen. Much more beautiful than real people. Sometimes he has sort of flowing white clothes, but usually he doesnt have clothes at all. And he knows all about me. And he always knows what to say. And he's always kind and gentle. And he's not like other grown-ups. Because he always tells me the truth. About everything, I mean. And he always knows what I want. And one day, he says, he's going to come and take me away to 'heaven'. He didnt say 'heaven' but I think that's what he means. But every time we begin to go up really high, I get frightened and have to make myself come back to where I'm sitting on the bed. But one day I will go with him forever, he says. He says I'll know when it's the right time. He's my best friend, but of course it's a secret. No one knows about him. Not even mummy.

Now I'm in the kitchen. Mummy gets in a bad temper when she has to do things in the kitchen. She tells me I get under her feet. I'm pretending to be mummy, cooking the breakfast. 'Oh damn the thing! Damn and blast the thing! Stay there, when I put you there, will you? Oh dear! I'm not cut out for this . . . ' Daddy's always going in and talking to mummy when she's cooking, and then gets cross when she shouts at him. But after he's gone to work, mummy starts whistling. Then she isnt in a bad temper anymore. I think mummy wishes she was like daddy and could go to work every day. Daddy's never in a bad temper. He goes away in the morning, and when he comes home in the evening, he's always glad to see me. But mummy tells him how tired she is, and gets very cross if he doesnt listen. Then they argue and shout at each other and, sometimes, daddy bangs the door and goes to the pub. Then mummy cries and says she hates him. But she doesnt hate him really.

I'm fed up with pretending to be mummy now. I'm going to go back to her bedroom and take all the greasy stuff off. I wonder why mummy doesnt play at being someone else. Then she could do anything she wanted. She could *pretend* that she had to go out. She could *pretend* that she had an exciting job, and lots of money. She could go to Abroad. She could take photographs and print them in books. But she doesnt do it, so maybe she *likes* pretending to be daddy's wife.

I've taken all the stuff off again now. I've put all the little bottles and jars back where they were, so mummy wont know what I've been doing. There's an envelope on mummy's dressingtable with daddy's name on it. I didnt notice it before. It's open. I wonder if it's got anything to do with the special parcel she's gone to get. I'm going to read it. She wont know.

It says: 'It's the only way. I'm sorry. Please forgive me.'

I've just heard mummy coming in the front door! It's too late to run down the stairs and out the back door. I'll just have to keep quiet and hope she doesnt come upstairs. I think I'll try and hide in my room.

I've just looked over the bannisters and seen mummy. She's got the special parcel. It's very *small* for such a *special* parcel. And it's all done up with brown paper and string, like a birthday present. She's taken it into the front room. I can hear her undoing it. I'm frightened. I wonder what it is. I know she'll be cross with me, but I'm going to go downstairs anyway.

'*Mummy! Dont! Please dont!*'

I'm alone in the house. Mummy's gone to heaven and I'm in my room on my bed. I'm sitting with my eyes shut and waiting for the beautiful young man to come. There he is. He's so beautiful! He's smiling at me. He loves me and I love him. He's taking me by the hand. We're flying away. Higher and higher. And this time I wont be frightened. I wont need to make myself come back. Because mummy's there already. She'll be waiting for me to come. She'll be happy at last. And we can be together.

Poor daddy! Now he's the one who's going to be alone in the house.

BLIND DATE

by Peter Robins

The doors hadn't closed. It was still not too late to cross to the other platform and go back. Back, inevitably, to the Common and a wary amble under the hawthorns. The Common was his hunting ground and adrenalin pumped at the mere notion. January or July — it made no difference — he could sense a blond at two hundred yards on a moonless night. Yet even if he did draw blank, find no one worth bedding, it was no matter. Tomorrow would be a very different day. Dear old Portsmouth for a lively weekend: his usual understanding landlady off the Commercial Road and a carefree round of the Bonjour Matelots. And so why the hell then this foray on a sour November night? For what? For whom? Twenty to one it would turn out to be a prancing ninny with bleached hair, a cleft palate, a sparrow's brain and crabs as a souvenir.

The doors closed uncertainly and it was next stop Lambeth North. How could any balanced intelligent being, Alan reasoned, have let himself be cast in this charade? Advertise for a flat, certainly; for a car, perhaps. To offer oneself, though, even from the anonymity of a box number as a man seeking another man? He'd allowed himself to drift into the ranks of the daft and the desperate. Rationalising the whole exercise could go on until Doomsday. There was still no glossing the truth. He, Alan Sanders, had put himself on the meat market and was no different from that lonely legion on the nightly quest for a relationship.

It was slim comfort that he'd eliminated thirty-seven of his forty answers. Posses of kinks and pensioned rent-boys had plopped on his mat in a rainbow of envelopes. He'd been astounded at the readiness of people to peel a photograph — full frontal in most instances — from a handy stockpile and rush it off to any faintly relevant advertiser.

Bill had been an easy first choice. The letter had been plain and direct. There was no artifice in the single sheet pulled from a commonplace writing pad. A skilled manual worker living in South London. Someone who liked a drink and a game of darts at the local. Alan felt there was no coy pretence in the explanation that his advertisement had been found by accident in a magazine bundled with some colour supplements outside the next bedsitter when the owner had flitted. We'll just see if he's prompt — or if he even materialises — thought Alan bounding up the emergency stairs that stank, as always, of cider and stale piss. It was four minutes to eight and Lambeth North looked just as forlorn as it had done when he'd passed through on the way to weightlifting sessions a couple of years previously. At the last turn of the stairs Alan reminded himself of the need to assess all loiterers smartly. If Bill was a bleached clown or clone, he had to be passed without the flicker of a question. Rain or no rain there was at least a handy pub.

Three people were waiting. A seventeen-year-old with a Labrador. Alan had long since concluded that there were others better equipped than he to cope with emotional virgins so, if Bill was the teenager, he'd a long wait ahead. The sad soul in the plastic cycle cape? Could that be Bill, so myopic that the glasses he fingered contorted his face to a fixed sneer? Sorry, thought Alan, and unobtrusively took in the third.

He was between the ticket window and the phone booths and could just be sheltering until the rain eased. Again, he could be waiting to see who turned up on a blind date. Alan looked at the rain and made it obvious that he'd paused to light a cigarette. The teenager hadn't moved or glanced. The man in the cycle cape had plodded to the top of the stairs. The man by the phone booths shook out a cigarette and glanced a second time. A Londoner without doubt, Alan felt. The high cheek bones, fresh colouring, broad unlined forehead and almost squashed nose were features to be seen any day in East Street and Balham market even after centuries of random breeding. The curly hair was, had to be, prematurely grey for the man couldn't be more than thirty-two or -three. The mid-blue eyes were beginning to twinkle and Alan realised he'd looked too long to be disinterested. Well, he thought, the evening may be worth more than a pair of sodden shoes. He moved easily towards the phone booths.

'Hello. I'm Alan.'

'Oh yeah . . . '

'You *are* Bill, aren't you?'

'That's right.'

The man didn't move. No handshake but the lips, the whole mouth, smiled.

'So,' Alan stubbed out his cigarette with a damp heel, 'what do we do? stand around until they lock us in for the night?'

'What d'you suggest?'

'This is your manor. What's the beer like on the corner? Unless you've got a crate at home . . . ?'

'Bit noisy that one. The mods have been moving in. So what makes you think I've stocked up special then?'

'If you invite someone over when it's pissing down, I reckon at least you get a few cans in.'

'There could be a few in the fridge. So, what do we do, nip back and watch the box?'

'Look, if you've dragged me from a warm Streatham flat to play coy at a dreary bloody tube station, let's forget it. I did have thirty-nine other replies to my ad.'

'Did you now? I should be so popular. Hold on. Put yourself in my place. You'd play for time a bit, yes? The room's not much but it's mine, see. No point in getting the push through taking some crank back, is there?'

'Ok, ok; sorry. Now, I haven't done time. I'm not kinky. As I said in the advert, I'm a straightforward bloke who prefers men's company. What else do you want — references?'

'Easy, then, easy. D'you drink rum and coke?'

'Is that important?'

'It is unless you're buying. All there is till pay day.'

'I drink rum and coke. Let's go.'

'Rightie.'

'Bus?'

'Not crippled are you? Five minutes down the road. Know this part at all?'

'Vaguely. I used to go weightlifting at Morley five years ago.'

'Can't be bad. Keeps you in better nick than crouched in a bloody van.'

'I thought you said you did skilled manual work?'

'Did I now? That's just what I do do. On contract. Restaurant chain up West.'

'This rain's getting worse. Much further to go?'

'Smile, mate. Next turning's ours.'

It was a tall emaciated house thrown up as part of an unending terrace for Victorians who expected to find one drudge inside and one water closet in the yard. At least the waft of carbolic as they closed the street door behind them was sweeter than lingering cabbage. The second-floor front was pleasant enough. Orange curtains to the skirting, plain wall lights against plain olive walls; a rosewood table and a chesterfield not greasy from generations of lodgers.

'Horror film's starting if you want it on.'

'I wouldn't mind. I'm a sucker for vampires. Sorry.'

'You should be. It's the top switch. Standard model. Like me.'

'That could just be why I didn't walk straight out of the station . . . because you are a very standard model.'

'You mean you find that interesting? Can't think why. Enough rum?'

'Plenty . . . by the way, I should make a phone call.'

'The one on the landing's jammed. Asked them to clear it a week ago and we're still waiting. Aren't you staying then?'

'Staying? Oh, I don't have to go yet awhile. Where do you usually sit?'

'Me? Anywhere. The wife used to sprawl all over the couch so I'm used to the floor.'

'You were married?'

Bill smiled at the top of his glass.

'That throw you? She moved out a month back.'

'Getting a divorce?'

'What for? She went her way . . . '

'She didn't understand?'

'You've got it all wrong mate. It was me slow on the uptake. Came back one tea-time with a wrenched ankle, didn't I, and caught her at it with the student downstairs. That was it. Finish.'

They watched the film, one at either end of the chesterfield and Alan conscious of the chasm of silence between them. He was distracted a little by the need to make that phone call. Unless he did so before midnight plan X would go into operation. The standard arrangement with his flatmate was that should one go out on a blind date or on the hunt, the other would stay in. If the All's Well call wasn't made then the stay-at-home would contact the police. It had never happened but Alan only half-concentrated on the terrors of the storm-swept castle as he speculated where the police might start a search: the lower Thames? Dollis Hill station . . . ? Primrose Hill . . . ?

'Sorry?'

'I said, have another?'

'Thanks. Steady on the rum though.'

'You were miles off.'

'Oh, just thinking how comfortable it is here.'

'Must be the company.'

'It could just be.'

Bill settled again and seemed intent on the film. It's now or never, thought Alan: we're at the point of no return. Married; divorced . . . what the hell? All that's for the sociologist and the pigeon-hole suburban mind.

Pulling a cushion from the middle of the chesterfield, he slid down onto the rug. Bill made no comment. Didn't stir. Alan moved his rum to his left hand, finished his cigarette and leaned back to stub it out without fully turning his head. As he brought his right hand down again he rested it on Bill's ankle.

'This the one that was wrenched?' he asked with every appearance of carelessness.

'Yeah but it doesn't hurt now.'

Which could mean that it didn't need massaging, however gently. Or again it might be intended to convey that Alan needn't be too tentative. Whatever it signified, he moved his finger-tips lightly but surely through the soft hair above Bill's instep. As he touched the calf there was a mildly funny moment in the film. They both laughed too quickly and then Bill moved for the first time in ten minutes, casually easing his leg at an angle so Alan could quite naturally let his fingers saunter further to the inside muscles of the thigh.

'Must go for a slash. Hold on.'

'Now what?' Alan muttered to the ceiling. An eleventh-hour bout of nerves and guilt? Surely not a sermon on sin, a cup of thick cocoa and a manly handshake? It could be worse — it had all been because Bill's wife had gone and another man was cheaper and more certain than wining and dining the scrubber from across the landing. Perhaps, just perhaps, the explanation for Bill's hasty exit was as simple as his statement, he'd gone for a piss.

Bill stood inside the doorway.

'Don't need all this light really,' he grinned, 'enough from the box.' He flicked the switch and then pushed the catch on the door.

He sat easily on the rug beside Alan with his back against the chesterfield. A moment later his left arm was along Alan's shoulder.

It is our fingers and our lips that talk — eagerly, reflectively and then as eagerly again — when we make love. The territory of a stranger's body is always crammed with wonders: contours, caves and slopes to be explored. Experience brings, as it does to the explorer, technique. Yet only the very lonely and the most naif can be deceived by skill alone. Without affection and concern there's no enduring pleasure and we recall such meetings with contempt.

Alan and Bill's meeting was punctuated by hugging and

caressing that signalled contentment and delight. They spoke only once. Alan edged his hand further and deeper between Bill's thighs until there was a sharp contraction of muscles.

'I don't.'

'Ok, ok,'   Alan murmured soothingly. 'Nor do I.'

'So?'

'So . . . there are other ways,' Alan whispered. 'Anyway, give me those that will face me.'

'Give me how much?'

'Doesn't matter . . . now, like this . . . yes?'

'I'll say. I like it; I like it. What about you?'

'I'd just say it's bloody wonderful.'

The film had ended when they lit the best cigarette of the day. Their heads touched on one cushion. Their bodies made a right angle.

'Your name really is Bill?'

'Fine bloody time to ask. Told you it was, didn't I?'

'Just wondered. Some invent names after dark you know. You must admit you were a bit odd though, back at the station.'

Bill laughed, caught his breath on the cigarette and spluttered. 'Bound to be, wasn't I?'

'You're telling me you haven't been with many men?'

'Oh, couple of times, years ago. Youth hostelling. Bit of the usual slap and tickle. Didn't mean anything really.'

'So what were you laughing at just then?'

'Thinking what a common old name I've got, I reckon. There's you wandering up at Lambeth North dead cool saying "Your name Bill?" and next to no time we're bollock naked on the landlady's prize Wilton. Bit of a laugh though, you've got to admit.'

'I don't see why. You'd hardly have answered the advert, come to meet me and expected us to talk about the price of fish fingers.'

'What bloody advert? Our phone's out of order, I told you. I was waiting to use the call-box. It's like I said, Bill's a common old name.'

CHRYSALIS

by Ian Everton

When Alan Tyndal met Martin Ryalls he had a very strange tale to tell. Ryalls reckoned that he had met Jimmy Ellis in a bar. They went back for the night and started to see each other on a regular basis, going to meetings and socials and becoming more involved. As Ellis had a bedsitter and Ryalls a huge house all to himself, Martin asked Jimmy to move in with him.

It couldn't have been better. After six months it was as though it had always been like this. Until, that autumn, the weather seemed to affect Jimmy unduly. He didn't want to go out to meetings and socials. Martin decided to go on his own, often coming home to find that Jimmy had not moved from the spot he had left him in, usually asleep in odd places, not just the floor or halfway up the stairs, but even in the bath tub. He said it made him feel secure. He would fall asleep anywhere if he wanted and there was nothing Martin could do about it. Well there wasn't. And other than this minor eccentricity what did it matter if he stayed in all the time? He never objected to Martin going out or even bringing someone back, as many as one a week. They were not against the idea of a ménage à trois.

Then Jimmy changed. He still stayed indoors and his sleep periods grew longer and longer; but he seemed to take a delight in beaming at his fingertips, drawing imaginary lines in the air and then nodding off. Martin began to wonder if it was time Jimmy should get in touch with a counselling group or, better still, that he should do so himself. He would have a party, bring lots of people into the house.

Jimmy found that he could produce thin membrane from his fingers at will. It was no more than a magician's trick, however much of an oddity, and at first Martin found it entertaining; but it wasn't all *that* good. He was more disturbed by Jimmy's constant reference to the following spring and the real him that would be revealed.

By now it was winter. Not really the mood for parties and bringing people back. He almost did, but his companions for that particular night decided to go to a club instead. Martin didn't go with them. He was wearying of the people he knew, and of Jimmy. Yet he wanted to be back home with him.

He found him in the outhouse. Jimmy had even brought a paraffin heater in. 'I'll want it on all winter', he said.

'Are you moving in here?' Martin asked. Jimmy gave him a look of disbelief. He had advanced his conjuring trick to making a small sack out of his cobwebs that hung from a shelf about eight feet from the floor. He had been intent on it all that evening since Martin had gone out. Nothing would bring him into the house. He said he had eaten enough earlier on — in fact Martin had watched him grow fat. And Martin left him there spinning the membrane which was now extending from the shelf down to the floor, hanging some few inches above it.

The next day Martin knew something was wrong. He could feel that things weren't the same. The house was cold and quiet. It had snowed. Birds and animals were not making their usual sounds, the last of the insects had disappeared some time before. Jimmy was still in the outhouse. He had been there all night. Nothing in the house had been taken. What if he had gone into one of his forty-eight-hour sleeps again?

Martin rushed over to the outhouse, uncomfortable in the new wave of coldness that the snow had brought with it. Inside the hut it was very warm. The paraffin heater was only half empty and, oddly enough, Martin remembered Jimmy's request that it should be kept on all through the winter. Up in the corner of the dingy room was hanging what appeared to be a huge chrysalis, nearly eight feet long and enveloping a form that might have been Jimmy.

That was the story Martin Ryalls told Alan Tyndal. It was why he preferred him not to go to the outhouse, and it was why he went across every day to fill the paraffin heater and make sure 'everything was alright'.

They had met at a Xmas party. Martin said he needed to get out of himself. People still asked where Jimmy was. And when Martin said to Alan that it was not true Jimmy had left him, and when they went home together and got on so well, he just had to tell him. Alan saw his tale as something symbolic. He needed to weave it to get over Jimmy leaving him. There really had been such a person, everyone knew that. Otherwise Martin was perfectly rational. Alan was going to give him what he wanted.

He hardly needed to be asked to stay. Like the other one, Alan had been in a bedsitter, not for long, but long enough to take to such a huge house. Martin continued to go to the outhouse every day, meticulous that the deliveries of paraffin were made; enough to last for months, even assuming the harshest of winters.

But a harsh winter it was not. Except that Martin caught a touch of the flu from some night-club. Alan nursed him, looked after him closely.

'But the outhouse,' Martin said. 'You must go and fill the heater every day. I'm too ill. If you don't, I will.' For the first time in their relationship Alan had the strangest feeling that — somehow — Martin actually meant what he was saying. This had never occurred to him before. He was in a situation where, because of Martin's flu, he was expected to continue this fantastic ritual every day as though the story had been literally true. It irked Alan. Normally he didn't mind. He enjoyed a bit of fantasy on the side, people needed rituals of some sort, but there was a point where you could take it too far.

He couldn't really refuse Martin's pleading request. Well it wasn't so much a request, it was more an order. It would not take many minutes to go into the hut every morning and make sure that the paraffin heater was full — if there was one there at all, of course. Martin told him where to find the key to the huge padlock that kept people out; he told him how to switch off the burglar alarm, which until now Alan had not even been aware of. It struck him that for all this time he had completely ignored the fantasy. He had never questioned it, and what's more it had never occurred to him to look in the outhouse for himself out of respect for Martin's wishes.

Alan turned off the alarm as instructed. Went into the hut, closing the door behind him immediately as told, in case Martin just might have been watching from a window. It was a dirty, shabby place, and the warmth hit him in the face. Insects were using it as a winter refuge. They were flying all over the place, more species than he could possibly count. And over in the corner he saw what appeared to be an old sack. Of course that was just what it was. But Alan had not been aware that Martin had taken the fantasy to this extent. It had never seemed necessary to . . . well, *make one.*

He filled the heater up, looked round at the window, at the door and over to the sack. He might as well just look. But it couldn't be, he thought, it was unthinkable. What if Martin had killed his friend, by accident no doubt? But the strain had been so much that he had put his body in the sack and created this netherworld that embraced two different orders of nature, the insects and the mammals. He could not look at the sack. And yet he must. What if Martin was suddenly better the next day, and he would never have the opportunity again? He had to find out. He had to be sure that it was not *his* mind that was playing tricks, now that he was in the reality of the situation, almost face to face with Martin's private nightmare after all these weeks.

It did look like an old sack — possibly with buttons for eyes. It was even the right general shape for a human being, though rather tall. Had Jimmy been hunch-backed? So far everything fitted in with everything else. He still did not know the true version of the story. Either Martin's need to fantasise, Alan's new hypothesis that he didn't want to be true, or the third, the account Martin had given him on their meeting.

There was only one way to determine which was the case. If it were a body it could not harm him. But it could! What was he going to do if Martin had accidentally killed Jimmy? He would not report it of course; he would comfort him, and admit eventually that he had guessed the truth. But what then? What were the two of them to do with the body? What in a few weeks, in a few years, if *they* came to the door enquiring about a missing person? And the people in the group — they constantly asked if anything had been heard from Jimmy. He couldn't face them. He and Martin would leave town as soon as he was well. They would get rid of the body, make a new start where there had never been a Jimmy. But he still had to take one look at the sack to make sure that it was true. Otherwise Martin would suspect *his* sanity, and not the other way round.

Alan touched the sack. It was made of a hard membrane with a homogeneity of its own from tip to tip. He felt its tough yet smooth texture, and putting his ear to it he fancied he could hear a slow beating. Very mild and deceptive at first, but after a minute or two — he didn't know how long he'd been in the hut — it was a definite, cosmic rhythm that he could recognise. It was alive.

Before going out of the hut for the first and possibly last time, Alan turned to look at the thing again. He had probably been in there half an hour. Martin might ask him what he had been doing. If the story was true ... if the story was *true*? He had to go back for a minute to check that it hadn't been his imagination. That the thing, whatever it was, was truly alive in some sense that he could understand. It was not a dead body in a sack. The thing was a law unto itself, a law he could not comprehend.

It was different the second time. He felt a lump in his throat. It was as if he was intruding on someone or something in its sleep that might wake up any moment, fierce at being disturbed. It was alive. There was no doubt. Now he had to get out. He felt sick and almost in a panic set about bolting the door, leaving the paraffin can inside the hut and forgetting to turn on the burglar alarm. Whatever it was, it was not human. It had never been human, and Martin had been nursing this ... chrysalis throughout the winter with some intention, with some hope, that it would turn into something. They would have to get rid of it. It was not Jimmy; Martin had lied. They had to get rid of it.

The best policy was to say nothing. Alan had been quiet all day, hardly touched his food as Martin tucked in, a sign of a speedy recovery. When he spoke out of necessity Alan could not hide the tremor in his voice. He felt cold, dared not look directly at Martin, who seemed to think that everything was the same as it had always been. It was not the same, how could it be? How could he act so normal with that ... ? And yet, as far as it went, this was nothing new to Martin. It was he who had harboured the animal. He who had kept the heater on for months to keep the huge brute alive. There was no reason why Martin should suddenly think that reality had altered its properties overnight. But he had said nothing. Had it not occurred to him that Alan had looked? Anyone in his situation would have looked out of curiosity. It would only be human.

In the evening Martin noticed that Alan had been quiet, but didn't seem to have any idea of the cause. He was feeling much better. Why, they might even go out for a drink the next evening. Really? He was better. It meant that the next day he would probably be able to fill the paraffin heater himself.

'What do you think of him then?' Martin suddenly asked. Alan started at the question. He had been trying to think up ways of approaching the subject all day without any success.

'What do I think of him?'

'Yes. Jimmy. You must have looked. You were in there long enough.'

'Martin,' Alan stammered and rose from his chair. Pointing in the direction of the hut, he said: 'That ... is *not* Jimmy.'

Martin burst out laughing at this. He was recovered from his flu by now.

'Of course it's Jimmy, what did you think it was? A moth?' Disoriented by Martin's unexpected behaviour, Alan gaped at him, feeling like a spokesperson for the rest of the human race.

'That thing,' he said in a high-pitched voice, 'is *not* human!' Martin gave a little laugh. Alan could not see what was funny, he had never acted like this before.

'I never said it was, did I?' Martin said, looking round the room as if there was someone there to answer his question. Alan sat down again. A joke was a joke was a joke. He didn't like it. He didn't like Alan's new mannerisms, as if he was turning into a different sort of person altogether. He had been suffering from flu of course, and that usually made people feel off. He wasn't himself. Perhaps in the morning; but why the morning? Alan couldn't sleep in the house with that creature out there in the shed. It might break loose and go on the rampage smashing things up, it might even kill. And it would be Martin's fault. He had to be stopped.

'I want to know what that is, where you found it, and what you intend doing with it,' Alan demanded.

'Tut-tut-tut-tut-tut,' said Martin. 'Calm yourself, relax. Have you no compassion for people who are different from yourself?'

'Different from *me*?' Alan said. Martin just smiled at his frustration. He didn't have to tell Alan anything if he didn't want to. And in all this he had some sort of a plan. He was going to let the beast loose in spring and he would prevent Alan from stopping him, that was obvious.

'What will it . . . look like?' Alan asked after fifteen minutes of sulking, while Martin finished off enough food for both of them. Martin looked up at him as though he had said something quite extraordinary.

'It will look like Jimmy of course. It won't look like someone else.' Alan was tiring of this. He made out he was going to bed. That was where he was going, but not to sleep. He could hear Martin downstairs playing loud music.

Alan woke up early in the morning. He realised he would have to do something fast. He had to talk to someone. What was the use? The whole thing was absurd. They could continue living together as before. If the thing was Jimmy they could have a ménage à trois. If it was a monster it would gobble up a few people and eventually the army would have to destroy it. What would it look like? He wondered at Martin. Things had changed now. He had not come to bed. Martin was up to something and Alan had to find out what it was. He slipped his clothes on, trying to be as quiet as he could, and came downstairs to what seemed an empty house.

Outside in the bleak winter night, stars clear, even a full moon,

the thing was still in the hut. Martin had not been out to it because
he would have left footprints in the snow. Alan went out to check.
Since nothing was logical, why should Martin leave footprints?
He might have flown. But the hut was as he had left it. The
paraffin can was inside and the burglar alarm had not been
switched back on. Martin could not possibly have been there. He
dared not look over to the chrysalis, which he was sure must have
been watching him with the most primitive of senses. He picked
up the can, switched on the alarm, locked the door and went back
into the house.

As he came in he noticed a trail of cobwebs that led to the cellar
door. They had not been there before, and they had not been made
by the usual kind of spider. Opening the door to the cellar he saw
the light was on. This must have been where Martin had gone.
Alan wondered at his own safety, like the moment he first thought
Martin had killed Jimmy. That had not been true. But after
Martin's strange remarks he wasn't sure if he ought to go down
there. Down he went, however, into the cellar, which he saw anew
although he had often been down to see to the coal, and take   up
the wine when Martin asked him to. And over in the cellar corner
was a chrysalis almost identical to the one that had been left in the
hut. This time he did not feel to see if it was beating. He had made
his mind up, he was getting out that night. He thought ahead
inductively. As things stood, the paraffin heater in the hut would
go out. Presumably Thing One would die, while Thing Two here
in the cellar . . .

What was all this? He had thought of him as his lover for the
past couple of months, the first he'd had in his life. Was he now to
think of him as a thing? A chrysalis to be compared with the animal
he'd encountered in the hut, out of the way preparing for spring.
Alan had felt for Martin. And Martin had felt for Jimmy. What
was the difference? Why had Martin not told the whole truth? But
then he had, except for this. He did not say he knew *why* Jimmy
had become withdrawn, only that he had. He did not say he didn't
know why. Because to him, to these . . . people, it was a perfectly
natural thing. How long had it been going on? How many of them
were there?

Alan knew he could not leave. He had to stay. He had loved
Martin like no one else before. He had a duty to perform. And he
would do it faithfully. Fortunately the temperature in the cellar
was no problem. It was the one in the hut that needed heating, he
would continue with that every day.

When Jimmy was ready it was Martin's turn. Then Jimmy and

Martin were together for a while watching over Alan who had chosen the attic. By summer the house was presumed abandoned. There was a will that passed everything on to the local gay centre. The three had made their decision. On a moonless night spreading their wings they took off in a northerly direction, not stopping until, tired, they reached the Scottish highlands; far from people, for that was what they were not. Happiness depends on circumstance.

SWITCHBOARD

by Eric Presland

I look at my watch. Nine thirty. Only another half-hour to go. I yawn. What a drag!

It's been a quiet evening. I look down the list of callers — only four since seven o'clock. Two wanted to know about gay pubs and clubs in Oxford. Well, that's easy. There aren't any. At least, not since the Red Lion changed hands. There's the King's Arms, I suppose, but that's mixed and reeks of student posers. The only identifiably gay bit is the CHE knitting circle, which will probably be talking about the choristers at St. Mary Magdalene. Hardly the place to send a forty-year-old radiator salesman.

What next? Oh yes, the silent caller. Probably a girl. Hope she rings back on Thursday when Brenda's on. And, to round the evening off nicely, an abusive 12-year-old who phoned three times in succession:

'Would you like my prick up your bum?'

'Not today, thank you.' Slam. Phone rings again.

'Are you bent?'

'I'm gay, yes.'

'Fucking poof.' This time he puts the phone down. Five minutes later, it rings again.

'I'm wanking.' (He giggles helplessly. So does his friend in the background.)

'That's nice. I hope you're enjoying it.'

He whispers to his friend, and they both giggle again. He comes to the phone again. Choking with laughter —

'My friend's wanking too.'

'Well, I hope you'll be very happy together.' More whispers. Helpless convulsions, and the phone slides back on the receiver. I never really know how to take these calls — how seriously, I mean. Maybe one day he'll ring back without his friend. Without laughing. . .

Not much to show for an evening. Just think, I could have been sitting bored in the King's Arms instead, comparing cassocks.

The ashtray is piled up with cigarette stubs. God, have I really got through that many? I must try and cut down. Trouble is, I'm as nervous as most of the callers, more nervous than some. If only they could see this place from the other end of the line. Like that devastatingly cool and flirtatious fifteen-year-old calmly discussing the relative merits, if any, of the Boltons and Coleherne, and me trembling like a junket with Parkinson's Disease in this grimy little room. How do they manage it? Where do they get that shaming certainty from?

What was it he'd wanted to know? Oh yes, the usual. 'Where's the nearest place to meet people my age?' I forget what I said. Should have given him the dates of the next Bay City Rollers tour, I suppose.

That's the trouble, really. It's all very well saying, 'Come Out, be positive, be gay and live a gay life,' but what are they meant to Come Out *to*? They could go to London, and be ripped off in the pubs and clubs there. The lucky ones mostly do. But round here? To CHE, to be stunned into apathy by committee, or to the Church to be preached at. Pity GLF folded. Not that they had much to offer the embryonic Comer-Outer. It's hardly anybody's idea of emotional support to be plunged into discussions of picketing Smith's or Marx's theory of value. No wonder nobody new ever came — well, not more than once.

Just look at the so-called diary. CHE coffee evening once a month, Gay Women's social ditto. The Church every Sunday. And that's about it. Not even a list of contacts you can go and talk to if you're fed up. Just a telephone number between seven and ten. As if you can time loneliness and frustration to fit in with office hours.

What the hell am I doing here anyway? What right do I have? A sudden twinge of doubt and self-contempt. Only three years ago I was thrown into the most unimaginable (to me) misery and confusion because my best friend was about to get married. Only two years ago I was hovering uncertainly outside my first gay pub. Even now I still fight a guerrilla war against my inherited straight attitudes. Why should I be sitting here presuming to advise, counsel or just cheer up whoever happens to be on the other end of the line? The hopelessness of it all is devastating; one crackling and inefficient GPO line against three thousand years of Western Civilisation and the entire economic and social structure of the Western World.

CITI - H

You can't do much for most of them anyway; the ones who ring up in search of sex, where can they go? Only back to the cottage where they came from. The middle-aged ones who suddenly discover 'leanings' after twenty years of marriage, and what are they going to do, and no they couldn't possibly tell anyone, and my God, what if anyone at work finds out and what about the children and . . . Casualties of heterosexual propaganda . . . You could predict that conversation word for word.

The lonely ones, in small towns and villages like Wantage and Witney and Banbury and Bicester, not knowing anyone else, not wanting to come into Oxford (for what?), and could we send someone out? We couldn't. 'Move? But I've got a good job here. Good prospects.'

Two years ago . . . How far away it seems. Did it really take me an hour and a half to force myself into the Red Lion? Every time I made up my mind to go in, somebody walked past, so I ran away. I must have looked at the stills outside the ABC opposite at least twenty times. Eventually I darted in, only to be terribly disappointed. Everybody looked so ordinary. I don't know what I'd expected. Handbags, make-up . . . The queens had been very friendly, and I'd been — I am — very grateful for that, and because no one seemed very interested in that momentous occasion. After a while, I drifted apart from them, but more faces, more names, a few friends came to replace them. Then GLF for a hectic year before the collapse, and so to here. We stagger into 1974 with nothing very permanent to show for all that activity, it seems.

Except being thrown out of home, of course. At first, I'd always done a quick tour round the square before going into the Red Lion, just to make sure there was no one I knew around. You get like that when you live in the same small town as they do. Once I nearly died when, after all the precautions, I walked in to discover my father's bank manager sitting at the bar; on reflection, I decided that he wouldn't be too pleased to have it known that *he* was there, so we maintained a conspiracy of silence.

After a while, realising that sooner or later I was bound to be 'found out', I told my parents. Or rather, I told Dad — I never have found out what he told Mum. I don't quite know what I'd expected, but certainly nothing of the violence which followed. All the social cant about perversion, sickness, disease, stigma, Natural and Normal; all the fundamentalist cant of sin, evil and damnation came pouring out — from a man who was last at church on my christening. I left the next day. I still see my mother from time to time, furtively, meetings which almost invariably end in tears on both sides. I haven't seen my father for over a year.

Regrets? I suppose so, for hurting my mother, for not handling the situation better, but in a distant, abstract sort of —

The phone suddenly cuts in on my thoughts. A slight start, then a thumping round the heart. Hastily reaching for a cigarette, I breathe deeply, count four rings, and pick the phone up.

'Hello, Oxford Gay Switchboard. Can I help you?'

The pips seem to last for ever.

'Hello. Oxford Gay Switchboard. Can I help you?

Silence. Are they going to ring off? I hope it isn't going to take long, it'll be past closing time. A low, hesitant voice, almost inaudible through the heavy interference.

'Do you help people with . . . problems?'

'We try to. Depends on what the problem is, really. Can you tell me a bit about it?' My voice is now bright and self-confident. Too confident.

'I'm sorry. You'll have to speak up a bit. It's a dreadful line this end.'

'I've got this problem, you see . . .' The voice is no louder. Age? Impossible to tell, he's so soft. Quite well-educated by the sound of it.

'It's . . . I think . . . I think I may be queer.'

'What makes you think that?'

'I met this man . . . ' Another interminable pause. 'In this toilet . . . he exposed himself . . . He followed me out. He kept following me. Then I saw him again. We went to his car. After that I kept meeting him. Till he went away. God, what am I going to do?'

'What do you want to do?'

'What do you mean?'

'Did you enjoy it?'

'No. Yes. At the time. Afterwards I was so ashamed. It's so . . . disgusting.'

'And you've only felt like this about this man?'

'No. Since he went away, there have been others. I can't seem to stop. I tried. I didn't go out for a month. But now — I seem to keep finding myself there, outside the toilet. Automatically. I don't even remember going there.'

'And how long have you been doing this?'

'Well, there were things at school . . . mucking about and . . . things. But that's all. I'd forgotten about it all till . . . recently.'

'Recently?'

'About a year. Just over.'

Just as the talk is beginning to come more freely, the pips break in with mechanical violence. They stop; silence.

'Hello. Are you still there?'

'That was my last two pence. What am I going to do? What if my wife finds out?' There is panic in the voice. But a clue at last.

'Is there a doctor who can cure me? Pills, or something?'

'Doctors only cure people by taking away their feelings for anyone.'

'I don't care. I've got to do *something*.'

'You've never talked to your wife about your feelings?'

'I couldn't. I just . . . went for a walk this evening. We don't talk now. Not after . . . '

Another of them. The casualties. Why do they keep falling for it? Try to get rid of the feelings by rushing into marriage; hoping the feelings will just go away, so they can forget about them. He's probably old enough to be my father, and here I am trying to be some sort of magician. The depressing knowledge of the way the rest of the conversation will go sweeps over me.

'You don't think things can go on the way they are now? After all, you've managed for some time . . . '

'Oh no. I feel so — dirty. When I walk in the house afterwards. I lie down beside her and try not to think about . . . what happened earlier on. But I can't drive it out of my mind. I'm sure she suspects something. She must.'

'Why?'

'I'm sure. I can just — feel it. When you've been married as long as I have, you just know these things. The way she looks at me. Sort of begging. As if she was willing me to change my mind. To come back.'

'But you couldn't talk about it?'

'No. We don't talk. Not about anything important. We haven't for a long time. Not since . . . '

That silence again. Don't go. Please don't go.

'Since what?'

'No, we don't talk.'

'And you don't think she'd be able to cope with it?'

'She's all I've got left. It's something. I'm too old to make a fresh start. It would hurt both of us too much. She's been hurt enough already.'

'But you don't want to give up these — experiences?'

'I've tried. God, how I've tried, believe me. But I can't. So I thought . . . perhaps a doctor . . . ?' A small despairing sigh wafts down the phone.

Another pause. Thoughts race through my mind. In a minute,

time will run out, the pips will go, he'll hang up, another failure of ours, convinced that there is no way out. Perhaps he's right. Fuck it, there has to be hope. We can't go on being so helpless. He won't ring again.

'Look, it's difficult to talk over the phone, isn't it? Would it make any difference if we could meet and talk about it? You know, over a drink or something, we'd find it easier to chat.'

'I don't know : . . '

Have I blown it? Too pushy?

'What about meeting in a pub early tomorrow evening?'

'Oh, I couldn't do that. Someone might see us.'

'Not even an ordinary pub? I don't look very — conspicuous, you know.'

'No. I can't risk it.'

'Somewhere else then. Under Carfax tower. There's lots of people around, nobody will notice anything.'

'What about my wife?'

'If it's on your way home from work, you can just say you're going to be working a bit late.'

Grudgingly — 'Yes . . . '

'Six o'clock?'

'I don't know . . . '

'Six o'clock?'

'I suppose so.'

'You'll need to know me. I'll be wearing a blue denim jacket and brown cord jeans. I'm about six foot tall, brown hair, glasses.'

Shit, that could be anybody. I wish my wardrobe was better equipped. Still, at least it's inconspicuous. The pips go again. I shout over them: 'Six o'clock, Carfax. Ok?'

But the line is dead. I write the call up in the log:

> 9.40. Man, 50-ish, married. Cottaging for a year, doesn't know how to stop, doesn't know how to tell wife, doesn't want to come out. Meeting Carfax tomorrow 6pm. No very lively hope of success. Appalling line. Are we being tapped? What a boring evening. Nite nite. Alan.

And as I empty the ashtray and switch off the one-bar fire with a sense of relief (as usual), there is a small doubt in the back of my mind. Despite the hiss and crackle, the voice seemed vaguely familiar. If only they'd speak up. Lights out, lock up, and a quick dash to the King's Arms for last orders.

Ten to six. The High Street looks smudgy in the grey early

evening light of autumn, and a wind plucks fitfully at my jacket. I
hate this denim jacket, it's far too butch. I can't think why I said
I'd be wearing it.

Any minute now it's going to start drizzling. Anxiously I
look across the street at the people gathered waiting under the
clock-tower, and again at the faces passing me on my side of the
road. Why am I waiting opposite Carfax rather than under it? I
don't really know. In case it's a hoax, perhaps, though the call
sounded genuine enough. And the space under the tower seems —
exposed. Paranoia, the straight legacy, again.

I light another cigarette, and the little Roman figure in the
tower clock comes out of his house to strike the hour, a flash of
blue and gold in the gloom.

Which one is he? All the faces seem possible. Looking at them as
I wait, they all seem nervous, furtive and unhappy in the dusk. I
never realised before how sad most people look: heads down,
frowning, mouths drawn tight. I may not at the moment be
positively ecstatic to be gay, but I'm sure it must be utterly
miserable to be straight.

Oh Alan, that's naughty. I catch myself at it again, as a rather
sunburnt slim executive with a droopy moustache and big moist
eyes goes past. Secretly, almost subconsciously, I'm hoping that
this bloke is going to be one of the pretty ones. Not much chance
of that; the pretty ones don't need phone services, they always find
their own feet. It's only the ones with fallen arches and varicose
veins and stammers and dandruff on their collars who are driven to
us. Don't be a fool. Remember what he said. He's going to be
middle-aged and totally unremarkable, except in his despair.

He's not going to come. I know it. I pushed him too hard, he
didn't ever really want to come. It's almost dark now anyway.
Perhaps his wife stopped him. More likely he just chickened out.
Better give him another ten minutes or so, just in case. Let it go till
the half-hour.

Mmm, I wish it was that one — stop it, you idiot. It doesn't
matter now, it's another one lost.

Suddenly I notice a short, slightly dumpy man looking into the
window of a cheap carpet shop next to the tower. His collar is
turned up, and he has a peaked cap low over his head, so that the
silver hair just shows between the two. He could just be
redecorating. I suppose, but he certainly looks nervous. He keeps
darting little looks over his shoulder in the direction of the foot of
the tower. He's looking at his watch. It must be.

Shit, why didn't I notice him before? Why does it get dark so bloody early these days? I can hardly see him in the shadows at all. How long's he been there? Bugger.

Quickly I thread my way through the crawling traffic across the road, waiting halfway for the bus to pass. It's gone, and now the view is clear, I see the man turn out of the doorway and walk purposefully down the street.

Christ, I know that back. I know that walk. Suddenly the fragments all make sense.

I run across the street after the figure, arms wide. I catch him up and tap him on the shoulder. He turns, startled, expectant.

'Hello Dad.'

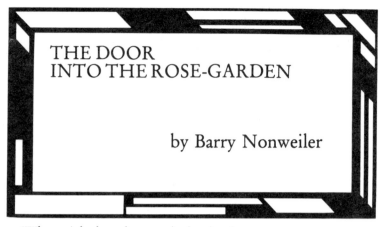

THE DOOR INTO THE ROSE-GARDEN

by Barry Nonweiler

'What might have been and what has been
Point to one end, which is always present.
Footfalls echo in the memory
Down the passage which we did not take
Towards the door we never opened
Into the rose-garden. My words echo
Thus, in your mind.'
                                   T.S. Eliot, *Burnt Norton*

Like the mass of men, Nick still found himself living a life of quiet desperation. This evening as he steeled himself to start handing out the leaflets, a gust of cold wind exploded on the picket line like a bomb, sending a debris of crushed and discarded leaflets and shrivelled brown leaves from the trees in Leicester Square scurrying past their feet like fleeing rats, sweeping a ragged smudge of angry charcoal-grey across the last glimmer of faded turquoise to the west, closing off the brief sunshine with the promise of winter as surely as the inevitability of deprivation and violence close off this time and place. 'This film exploits gay people,' shouted the young Scotsman beside him, brandishing his placard menacingly. 'Don't waste your money. It's all lies anyway.' Filled with a wishfulness for the same energy and confidence, Nick gingerly pushed a leaflet in the general direction of some Hyde-like juggernaut in a business suit, whose fat pink hand recoiled from the slip of paper as if it had been faeces. Nick winced with a kind of automatic childlike fear, and turned to catch the eye of the next person with a well-schooled patient resilience. It was a group of teenagers, one of whom with a half-hearted skinhead haircut and a blankly malicious gaze said 'Here you are, mate, have this,' and laying the flat of his hand against Nick's chest, shoved him back against the railings, where he banged the base of his spine.

The teenagers clomped on, laughing mechanically, with the one who had shoved Nick just silently grinning in his risen prestige. Nick straightened himself up and rubbed his back with his free hand. He caught a policeman watching him out of the corner of an eye.

'Did you hurt yourself?' said the Scotsman chirpily. 'Och well, it's all in a good cause.'

Minor violence hung loosely about the whole brief history of Nick's life, as if, he used once to think, by its very failure ever to be major or spectacular sealing the peripherality of such a life amid the real violence of the world about it and the times to come. As a child, his hypocritically moralistic father had beaten him cruelly with a belt, but not often. Though the very infrequency of the beatings gave them a peculiar horror. Once, not long after he had come out, in some despair for sexual contact he had allowed some friends to take him to Hampstead Heath: but the place terrified him, the nightmare-like corridor of trees prowled through by secretive and predatory married men, out to use and discard one another for the satisfaction of what was experienced only as a viciously repressed compulsion. Or so at least it had seemed to him then, and he had started to walk quickly away, only to find himself surrounded by a group of drunken young queer-bashers with bottles, who kneed him in the stomach, brought him to the ground and kicked him in the back, as he cradled his face with his arms and cried. But then unexpectedly they ran off, leaving him with nothing broken and not even an enduring scar. The only scar he had was where the fat middle-aged Cypriot cook who worked in the same snack-bar, who was always chucking him under the chin and blowing him kisses when he wasn't making demeaning and possessive remarks about every woman he could lay his appraising eyes on, had once with deliberate carelessness splashed him on the forehead with hot fat.

Such occasional isolated attacks seemed to Nick like the odd bursts of genuine hostility in the London winter, which for the most part was no more than a long niggling discomfort, grey skies bleached of hope but unmoved to fury. He tended to see it as no pure coincidence that recently the weather was becoming worse than for hundreds of years.

He stepped out boldly, and the jostling Saturday night crowd lurched uncaringly against him, or pushed him aside, driving on its way through pools of draining fluorescent light with a glazed

single-minded stare, eyes half-shut against the existence of other
people. But after a while he found to his excitement that he was
getting rid of a few leaflets, and even began stretching out, eager-
eyed, to more or less force them into people's hands. The
policeman came up to him then, and standing quite motionless
beside him, muttered into his ear 'Move back out of the way, mate,
or I'll do you for obstruction.' Nick turned and went back to the
railings, feeling the night wind cut through his light jacket, which
he had snatched up in a hurry as he fled from the house to catch the
vaguely twenty-past tube.

The disco-queen he shared a flat with had been standing in front
of his bedroom mirror, dressing for the night, as he ran past down
the hall. 'Should I wear Givenchy or Monsieur Rochas, now that
it's autumn?' he had called to Nick over his shoulder, looking at
him suspiciously in the mirror.

'I don't know, they're both nice,' said Nick, with an impatient
politeness, trying to make it look convincingly as if he could really
only pause for a moment.

'And where are you off to so fast on a Saturday after you've only
just got in from work?' asked his flatmate insinuatingly, making
arch eyes in the mirror as he unscrewed the perfume. 'Come on,
what's its name this time?'

Nick told him where he was going, feeling to his own discomfort
the usual rush of self-effacement that always came over him when
he had to explain his actions to his flatmate.

'Oh, how boring,' said his flatmate predictably, lightly patting
his cheeks with a very graceful motion. 'Why picket that film?
Why not just ignore it? Or go and see it? Oh well, byebye.'

Nick had been living with him for over a year now. He had
found the flatshare as the result of a rather desperate and
characteristically timorous phone call to Gay Switchboard. Yet
never for a moment would he deny that it was a great improvement
on the dreary bedsits in lonely houses full of sullenly introverted
straights where he had dragged out five or six years of his life since
finally leaving home, later than many. Just as his tedious job in a
snack-bar off Oxford St, the latest in a succession of similar jobs,
was an improvement of some kind on the aimless deprivation of
his days on the dole, which had followed an abortive year of
university in Leeds. Or so at least he told himself when the
arrogance of wealthy customers, or the anti-gay anti-woman abuse
of the cook, or the simple stench of hot fat clinging to his skin and
hair, threatened to become too much.

He often used to wonder why his flatmate had accepted him in the first place. But then he did not want much from Nick, it was enough if Nick was a silent but credibly sympathetic audience to his occasional monologues of unaccomplished holiday plans or five-minute heartbreaks, or more often, a kind of talking mirror that could reassure him that his latest clothes were all he hoped of them. When friends dropped in for gin and pâté or lovers blundered out bleary-eyed to the breakfast table, he would show Nick off as a kind of curio, something unusual that gave his home something others hadn't. For his part, Nick was glad to feel useful to another human being, in however marginal a way. He had a certain fluctuating regard for his flatmate's apparent blatancy, although Nick often used to wonder whether he was not protected as much as anything by a conscious aura of class, and after all, he never walked the streets at night, always being driven home or taking a cab. But Nick was fond of his ebullience, and sometimes he even found himself feeling a little wistfully envious of the apparently satisfying simplicity of the other's life, with its easy frivolous concerns and endless untroubled sexual play.

For himself he knew this world was one he could never enter, and never could have entered. Always, always he had been haunted by this vague obsessive longing, this belief in a world of intimate human relationships rooted in compassion and care, in sharing and creativity, although where it came from he had no clear idea. It was the very reverse of his background, the sterile loveless routine of his parents' relationship, and so far as he knew, it was a world that had had no existence on Earth for hundreds of years. More and more he had been caused to wonder whether such a hazy belief was foolish or misguided, and even to treat it as a shameful secret.

But there were times again and again when it struck him with the force of an instinct: it was what motivated his clumsy gropings towards political commitment, and above all, it was what he sought and — like most other people, he had come to think — failed even to come near in sex.

Standing back at the railings, Nick hunched his round shoulders and folded his arms across his chest, tucking the leaflets under an armpit.

'The sooner winter comes, the sooner it will be spring,' said a friend of his, a gentle little man with a big earring, shivering, but smiling warmly.

Nick smiled back wistfully. 'So winter come!' he quoted quietly, from an Edward Bond poem that someone — it would have been Huw, of course — had shown him somewhere once. 'That we may

see summer/ Before we are old.'
    'What did the pig say to you?' the big Scotsman asked Nick,
lowering his placard from above his head at last.
    'He told me to move out of the way, or he'd do me for
obstruction.'
    'They're looking for trouble, right enough, I can see it.'
    Nick was not sure, but he thought there were now more cops
around than when he arrived. He had a great recalcitrant fear of
being arrested. He knew that the abuse of the police would be no
uglier than that of the cook, that their beating would be no worse
than that of the part-time queer-bashers on the Heath. If he
looked for the roots of his panic, he thought he found them in the
quite rational horror that he had been born into a world roamed
through by human beings who, merely for what he was and what
he thought, could deprive him of his liberty or his property, could
lie about him, could physically beat him or even kill him, all
without even fear of reprisal.
    'Here, relieve me of this for a while,' said the Scotsman, handing
Nick the placard. 'I'll give out some leaflets for a change.'
    Nick handed him the leaflets and took the placard, which he
held in front of him, at a level too low, in fact, for most people to
read it. He watched the tall Scotsman stride out into the crowd
and shed leaflets into the hands of astonished passers-by as if they
were sweets, the pile almost visibly diminishing by the minute,
keeping up a constant patter of 'Come on, take one, they're free,'
and so on. He began to lope up and down in front of the picket-
line, and suddenly, in a quite ferocious roar, began a chant, 'Give
us a G! Give us an A!' By the time they got to Y, with a soft word of
encouragement from his friend with the earring, even Nick had
tentatively joined in. The high buildings all around added a distant
sympathetic reverberation in the neon-lit gathering darkness. As
soon as the chant was finished, the Scotsman, swinging his long
arms now in encouragement, was just launching loudly into a
chorus of 'We're here because we're queer,' when a short police-
sergeant with a black pencil-moustache tapped him imperiously
on the shoulder and, as the Scotsman lowered his head to listen,
said something inaudible into his ear. The Scotsman raised his
eyebrows, and came back to the line in silence.
    'He says there's to be no shouting or singing,' he said at large. 'I
suppose he doesn't want us to look at all happy.'

    Nick's life had changed enormously since he became involved in
the gay movement, and yet in some ways it had not changed at all.

His involvement had come slowly. He had been in his late teens, just out of school, when the first wave of gay liberation hit London. At that time, although he felt curiously warmed by its existence, and all too ready to speak out in its support, he never supposed it had anything directly to do with him. He was living at home, filling in time as an office temp, and going out with the same young woman, a friend of a friend, that he had been dating for the last eighteen months of school. She wanted to marry him, they liked one another's gentleness and the same music, and neither had had any other experience that caused them to think that the dispassion and awkwardness of their love-making was anything other than what was to be expected at first.

It was then that Nick first became really aware of his longing for a better world, for some other time that he might have been born into. Privately he put down his sexual dissatisfaction to this — as it seemed to him — purely abstract longing, this quirk, in fact; which was what must have been just as much responsible for that vague sense of difference he so often felt from his male schoolmates, not least when they were talking about sex.

The next year he went north to university, in a dark and bitter winter became at first curious about and then clumsily and uncomprehendingly involved in student politics, foresaw disinterestedly as the end of the year came that he was going to fail most of his exams, and as summer failed even to try and break through the endless washed-out cloud realised one empty Sunday afternoon in a fit of sheer panic, which seemed to lift him up like a lightning-strike and drop him half-dead on the ground, that he was alone. With an aimless suddenness, he decided to return to the kindly sun, the red bricks and somnolent green of the south-east, though he had no idea what else might be there. And then, a couple of weeks before he was due to leave, after spending a night in the pub with a man he had got to feel quite close to over the past few months, he found himself hugging and kissing with him, with a wonderful certainly that took him quite by surprise. They went to bed together a few times before Nick left. It was not the other man's first time, though he claimed he was bisexual. He was not very impressed with Nick's awkwardness, and Nick was perplexed by his own ignorance and diffidence. In retrospect, it seemed to Nick it was not the actual experience, lacking in anything like ecstasy as it had been, which had changed the course of his life, but the fact: that initial certainty of the contact of another man's body, like the certainty of water slaking long thirst.

Knowing that he was gay made many things fall into place, but so slowly. At first, returning to his parents' home, he had ventured out rarely and furtively to the few gay pubs he had heard of, which left him with a strange feeling of naivety. He hung back nervous and horrified, trying to merge into the sombre woodwork, watching a desolate, snatching, bitchy world he did not understand. On the odd occasion that someone sauntered over to try and pick him up, where he dangled sheepishly against a pillar or in a corner, he would swallow his drink, make some mumbled laughable excuse, and leave.

Finally he crept off to his first gay liberation meeting. Getting through the door was almost worse than going to the dentist, he had to remind himself quite firmly that he was an adult. Such a meeting was a pitifully small affair in London at that time. He sat, silent and a little bored, patiently listening to what was going on, which was mainly a dismal discussion of why the meetings were so small and what should be done. Much later, Nick had come to realise that this sense of its own decline, this endless fragmentation, could be found somewhere in the gay movement in London at any time, and was merely an element of its constant adaptation. On that first occasion, he had been on the point of leaving in painful disillusion, but had hung on with a kind of last-ditch resignation, until the meeting had moved off to a nearby pub, dissolving into intimate and resilient conversation, graciously and welcomingly subsuming him, to his own unimagined joy and relief. He embarked on a long discovery of self-respect, of his position in the structure of society, and at last a hesitant trust in the possibility of companionship.

He left home. The woman who had wanted to marry him wrote to him from Bristol, where she had been for the last ten months or so, half-apologetically, half-bitterly, saying that she had found what had been lacking in their relationship. He wrote back announcing joyfully that he was gay, but she never replied. He lay around in untidy bedsits, grubbing a life on the dole, groping for an understanding of the injustice all around him, reading *Marx for Beginners* or the odd copy of *Socialist Worker,* yet failing to find a reason for his own life in all that coherence. Then the gentle friend of his with the earring introduced him to the basic texts of feminism. His own oppression, his own longings slid ecstatically into their place, amid the grinding cogs of late capitalism. He felt transformed by knowledge and righteous anger, fuelled by these things alone. He got himself a job, to have money for books. He immersed himself now in sexual politics with the joyful relief that his life had at least a historical purpose, filling his diary with meetings and demonstrations.

And yet, and yet. He remained desperately sexually deprived. For a long time it had seemed he had dwelt in a kind of prison of insensitivity, shut off from the apparent pleasure which his body gave to a string of comparative strangers whom he had allowed and sometimes encouraged to take him, at alternative discos or benefit dances or wherever. Nine times out of ten, it seemed to him when he looked back on it, the man he had got off with would end up laying him on the bed, jumping on, noisily satisfying himself one way or another, then falling asleep: and if this was exaggeration, it was not a distortion. Usually, Nick would lie back and think of England: on his money, he had no hope of ever getting anywhere else. Once or twice he had summoned up the courage, out of some fondness or respect to the other, to talk about what they might do sexually, but this had only meant that they ended up doing nothing at all. He put it down to inexperience, but began to wonder when his inexperience would set him free.

And then, at first to his disbelief, he suddenly realised the rightness and the fulfilment of his physical feeling, not with anyone whom he had dutifully found attractive in some crowded mechanically erotic place, but with a gentle, passionately honest and rather timid man from Cardiff, who had been his best friend for months. He said nothing, because the reality of the relationship between them struck him with such obviousness that he could not believe it was necessary for him to spell it out. They continued as they had before, seeing one another three or four times a week, often talking long into the night, soothing one another's fears, stirring one another's dreams, learning from one another, sometimes ending up sleeping on the floor of the other's room, always turning up to meetings together, seeming to the outside world inseparable. Dazed by the intensity of closeness, the unexpected joy of caring for one another, Nick waited humbly for the inevitable moment when of their own accord their bodies would simply reify this unimaginable sympathy. But one night, when they had gone to a disco together as often before, Huw disappeared with a bikie. Puzzled, even incredulous at first, Nick decided to ignore the incident. Indeed nothing seemed to have changed between them, everything went on as before. But then it began to happen regularly, and soon Huw would have vanished for days with some tastelessly macho man before Nick saw him again. Nick did not feel jealous in any real sense, because he could not imagine that Huw shared anything with these men that he would have wanted to share with him. Despite himself, he did feel cheated, even betrayed. Sensing his resentment, Huw confided in him one night, in a tone that pleaded reasonably for understanding in a world of sexual repression and role-stereotypes, that he could only find himself sexually excited by sadomasochism.

At first Nick encouraged their friendship to struggle on, but it was like the spasmodic movements of a chicken after its head has been cut off. Hesitantly but inevitably, like some seasonal change, Nick's love turned at first into anger, then into hatred; and at last, merely into politeness, a sterile politeness that refused to set either of them free.

As time went by, he had found himself slipping back into the routine of casual encounters, but a sadder and a wiser man, knowing now to ask and to experiment, seeking to be whenever possible with the seemingly gentle, the seemingly hopeful, who suddenly seemed more and more at last to be around. But it was no good: for his part, all was swamped by the anxiety that he must cope with what remained the essentially consumeristic nature of such transient contacts, even at the time must ease them on their way by pretending to back-up resources of emotional richness he did not have. These people were men, after all, with all a man's expectations of owning and using the world in these times. Even those he might have liked would alight only briefly on his life and fly off, leaving it trembling. Whether it was the next day or the next month, feeling around the tender hollow left by the other, he felt himself finally even more destitute than before.

For nearly a year now, he had been avoiding even sexual contacts of this kind. The only affairs he had were those imputed to him by his flatmate, who refused to believe they were only a product of his voluble imagination. Nick was immured in a life of reluctant restless celibacy that had begun to feel as much like home as the hardness of our times: since both, he had come to understand, were a product of historical social forces outside his immediate effective individual control.

'I'll give out some more leaflets,' said Nick, leaning the placard against the railings. 'I'll go along the queue.'

A bearded drag-queen beside him efficiently split his pile in half, pushed the leaflets into Nick's hand, and steered him on his way with a light hand on the shoulder.

The faces in the queue were stiff, blank, uncaring. They looked through Nick as if he did not exist, as they would have looked through any human being, recognising neither kinship nor enmity. They were the faces of those who had acquiesced in the theft of their moral responsibility, who were beyond shame as they were beyond hope. They asked for little but the occasional sensual titillation which for a moment reassured them of the illusion of life, like the reflex of the tapped knee of a body in a coma. They saw little need even to defend themselves, not even bothering to raise a hand against the proffered leaflet, simply not seeing it.

Nick wandered back along them, and stood in the doorway of the cinema. On either side of him rose pillars plastered with glossy images of violence. Subtly corrupting images implying that all gays were violent. Uncommenting sensationalist images of violence against gays. Nick felt physically threatened by the very walls about him. Instinctively he rounded his shoulders as if to shield himself from a blow.

Across the pavement someone snatched the leaflets from the hand of Nick's friend with the earring and scattered them angrily in the air. The wind took them and blew some of them back in the zombie-like face of the man who had thrown them; his arms flailed, brushing them from him as if they had been verminous insects, one hand catching Nick's friend in the eye, as he blundered angrily on. A friend came up and put his arm tenderly round the man with the earring, gently offering a reality of consolation. Then they hugged one another, as if each deserved to be handled carefully, and briefly, softly, they began to kiss one another in gratitude and reassurance. Two policemen came up on either side of them, caught them in big, black, gloved hands, and bundled them away in silence, like sacks of rubbish. It all happened so swiftly and quietly that it was hard to believe it had happened to all.

'Look, they're arresting us! They're arresting us, just for showing that we're fond of one another!' screamed the big Scotsman. His voice was so loud, so grieved, it was as if he wanted it alone to shrivel the policemen where they stood. But no one in the queue seemed even to hear it. A couple from Hampstead on their way to the theatre turned vaguely to look in curiosity, and muttered something to one another, drifting on, pressed close.

Some confusion followed. The picket huddled in on itself, placards wavered and came down. Some people went off to phone lawyers, others to wait outside the police-station. They were a small group, what else could they do? Around them the remaining policemen waited like vultures, joking quietly with one another out of the side of their mouths.

A sound like heavy guns shook the air, flapping from side to side of the square like a moth in a lampshade. Starlings exploded from

the buildings and the trees, shrieking, wheeling against the brown
night sky, orange in the lamplight. A pinkish glow lit the skyline to
the south. It was fireworks for the Queen's birthday.

Nick felt dazed, drained. That we should be arrested for
showing affection to one another, by those protecting a film which
makes money out of violence against us, he thought.

'Let's go and get a drink,' said someone, and Nick drifted off
amongst them, faded remnants yearning for consolation. They
ended up in a pub in St Martin's Lane. 'And you'd better not kiss
here either,' a man muttered beside Nick, 'or they'll throw you
out. Some gay pub!' Nick pushed his way through the crowd
towards the bar, people turning on him angrily as he struggled
past, it was like an experiment on overcrowding rats in a cage.
Eventually an aggressive red-faced straight barman, who looked
like a butcher, got him his pint disinterestedly, if not grudgingly.
It wasn't even draught, only a fizzy solution of burnt sugar. With
difficulty he made his way back to the others, but he hardly joined
in their conversation. On every side, wherever one turned, tired
eyes rose as if pulled by a string and grabbed hold of his; eyes
without tenderness, without happiness, without hope; eyes of
those not hunting for sustenance, merely half-heartedly preparing
to consume because consumption was their self-definition. They
were like bleeding bulls, lunging again and again mechanically at
the empty cloak waved before their eyes, never lifting their heads
to see that in fact they were trapped.

And Nick was there too, his eyes going round the pub despite
himself; pitying, yearning, dreaming. This was the world he, like
the rest of us, must live in, in miniature. A world shaped by an
interpretation of sex as consumption, and not communication. A
world shaped by images of maleness as ownership, as aggression, a
fear of seeming gay, or even gentle, a shame at seeming poor, or
even unattractive, a compulsion to succeed. None of these things,
he wanted none of these things, and yet he could no more flee from
them now than he could ignore the way they had already marked
out for him what was to be done.

Nick turned away his eyes from the pub, and stared down at his
tremulous image in the surface of his beer. He no longer expected
ever to look in his mirror and see 'the lineaments of gratified
desire'. Instead he saw a brow furrowing with thought, a lip
curling in anger, eyes becoming hard with determination. This was
the only beauty of our times. In a world to come there would be a
time for love, a time for faces moulded by kindness and creativity:
for Nick, who dreamed of such a world as he might have dreamed

of a country left in infancy, from now into the imaginable future, like many, many others for whom the grip of our past seems like that of a drowning sailor trying to pull a survivor from a spar, for him only the harsh dignity of struggle.

He sat in the tube, pretending to read, unable to keep his mind on the page. But he tried to keep his eyes there so as not to have to look up at the bored queens on their way home, dutifully cruising the crowd like some compulsive pickpockets able to see people only as potential property to be stolen. He was swayed hither and thither, uncomfortably, inside the train's inescapable onward movement, through the darkness beneath the earth.

Suddenly he had that feeling as if he had been called, but called from afar, a different place, and as now his eyes rose, he became very slowly aware of the coffee-coloured black man in clothes that might have been American who had been sitting relaxedly opposite him, right opposite him, for a while now, and as he might least have expected, was looking at him; and he looked back, and did not, to his surprise, want to look away, because perhaps it was as if he saw, or no, as if they saw in one another some possibility, rising slowly, dimly, cautiously to the surface of their gaze; and when by some mutual agreement both looked apart, and looked about them, it seemed to Nick it was only so that their eyes might meet again and be now reassured that what they saw was something different. Nick stared along the carriage, seeking out all the other tired queens: who were looking at one another like the day before yesterday's cold meat they were sitting down to yet again. And his eyes came home to the black man's, where there opened like a flower such gentleness, such respect, such easy happiness: they lit another world like brown full moons high in a white sky; and his own eyes filled with such compassion. And Nick found himself beginning to smile, and as he did so, the black man's smile broke through too, till its light dappled all his face, for a moment so bright it should have dazzled, but did not. And they sat there on the tube, smiling at one another, their steady gaze like warm water washing and soothing one another's old wounds.

It was time for Nick to change, and as the train came to a stop he saw from the black man's stillness that he was not going to get off.

Nick tensed his body and stood. It was not important. The moment was complete.

As he joined the queue to leave, the black man said softly, graciously, with a kind of decent wishful sincerity, 'Goodnight.'

And Nick also said 'Goodnight,' one word, between what must have seemed to others complete strangers, to seal a new era, a new realisation that dreams might be hopes.

He shuffled through the crowd and climbed up the escalator. The moment was complete. They were happy simply in the knowledge that one another existed.

But when he got to the upper platform, which seemed as much at the level of reality as the level of the ground, and found his usual uncomfortable leaning-place waiting for him in the growing cold, while others sat together, or prowled to and fro in front of him, already the desolation of the present began inexorably to wipe all happiness away.

It was time for Nick to change, and as the train came to a stop he saw from the black man's stillness that he was not going to get off.

Nick tensed his body and stood. He could not help a certain regret that caused his eyes to gutter like a candle, and yet the black man still looked at him, calmly, joyfully. Perhaps, after all, the moment was complete. He joined the queue to leave.

The seat beside the black man had become empty, and he dropped lightly into it, as if it had happened automatically, saying 'Where are you going?'

The black queen's warm, soft hand closed gently round his, the tender fingers warming away yearning, gratitude and reassurance passing between the brushed silk of their palms, as slowly they rose, and knowing all one another's wants and lost hopes for the world in that one moment, looking unafraid into one another's eyes, laughing with one another, the black queen said 'I'm bound for paradise, man.'

And there in the crowd, they gently kissed, and then stood, their arms carefully about one another, while the escalator bore them slowly heavenwards.

Simon Burt was born in Wiltshire in 1947, and studied classics at Trinity College, Dublin. Since 1972 he has been teaching modern languages in South London. While continuing to write short stories, he is also at work on a novel.

Ian Everton entered the gay movement in 1971. He lives in Leeds with his lover, the artist Syd Leaf. His novel *Alienation* is also published by Gay Men's Press.

Robert Glück was born in 1947 and lives in San Francisco, where he runs writing workshops at a non-profit bookstore. His work has been published in *Gay Sunshine* anthologies, in *Body Politic* and in *Social Text*.

Sam Green has been a nurse, postman, small-town politician, community worker, seller of tat, hostel warden and unemployed. He lives now in London, but still gets homesick for Durham and civilisation.

Martin Haven grew up and came out in the Midlands but has lived for many years in London. After a long stint as a bus driver, he is currently unemployed, which he hopes will give him the time to develop his writing.

DuMont Howard lives in San Francisco, and has published in *Cineaste, Blueboy* and *Christopher Street.* He is working on a screenplay, and planning a book on female pop vocalists.

Adam Mars-Jones studied English at Cambridge, has taught in Virginia, and is at present living in London. A collection of his writing, *Lantern Lecture,* was published in 1981, and he is currently editing an anthology of gay short stories.

Barry Nonweiler was born in 1949 in South-East England, and bred in Belfast and Glasgow. He has been active in the gay movement in London, in New Zealand and in Australia, where he taught at university. His novel *That Other Realm of Freedom* is also published by Gay Men's Press.

Eric Presland was born in London in 1949. He got involved in gay politics in Oxford in 1972, and helped to start Britain's first Gay Switchboard there in 1973. He is a contributor to the anthology *The Age Taboo* (1981), and currently involved in the gay theatre company Consenting Adults. He also writes regularly for *Capital Gay*.

David Rees lives in Devon and teaches at Exeter University. He has written several novels for children and teenagers, including *Quintin's Man, In the Tent,* and the best-seller *The Milkman's on His Way,* which all have a gay theme. In 1978 he won the Carnegie Medal for *The Exeter Blitz,* and in 1980 The Other Award for *The Green Bough of Liberty.* His adult novel *The Estuary* is also published by Gay Men's Press.

Peter Robins' work has appeared in magazines in Britain, Holland, Sweden, the United States and Australia. Other books include *Doves for the Seventies* (poems; 1970), *Undo Your Raincoats and Laugh* (gay short stories; 1977), *The Gay Touch* and *Our Hero Has Bad Breath* (gay short stories; both 1982); and he is a contributor to the anthology *On the Line* (1981). He is a working journalist and lives in South London.

Alan Wakeman's published fiction includes the play 'Ships', written for Gay Sweatshop (in *Homosexual Acts,* 1975), *Tim, Willie and the Wurgles* (for children; 1976), *Hamun and Giben* (1978) and several stories for BBC radio. He has lived for many years in Central London.

Jon Ward studied English in Cambridge, social work in Brighton and silk-screen printing in Bradford. He came out in the mid-seventies when he was 24. He is currently writing a book about sex and language.

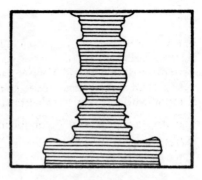

Gay Men's Press is an independent publishing project set up to produce books relevant to the male gay movement and to promote the ideas of gay liberation.

Other fiction titles in our list include:

Ian Everton
Alienation
A highly emotive novel from the gay movement, set in a gay group struggling for survival in a homophobic North of England city. Like their new-found friends, lovers Peter and Jon seek to make a better life for themselves; but the real and ideal worlds rarely coincide.

Barry Nonweiler
That Other Realm of Freedom
Glasgow, London and New Zealand form the backdrop to Simon's quest for freedom, in a novel that fearlessly holds a mirror to gay oppression. 'The reader will be dazzled by his intricacy and the extent of thematic concern' *(Gay Community News,* Melbourne).

David Rees
The Milkman's On His Way
Teenager Ewan Macrae's struggle for a positive gay identity is charted with sensitive frankness in this bestselling novel. 'A better account of gay coming-of-age is not to be had' *(Mister)*.

David Rees
The Estuary
Following the success of *The Milkman's On His Way* this prize-winning author makes his debut as a writer of adult fiction, exploring the conflicts in three relationships (homo- and heterosexual) among a group of friends. A novel for the eighties.

Giovanni Vitacolonna
A Sweet and Sour Romance
How do you keep a relationship going, or just your emotional balance, on the fast-moving gay scene of today? These are among Sal's problems as he plunges into the sexual whirlpool of San Francisco, then off in search of a new life in Italy. Sparkling, insightful and hilarious.

Gay Men's Press also publishes books in the fields of Art, Drama, History, Politics and Psychology. Send for our full catalogue to Gay Men's Press, P O Box 247, London N15 6RW, England.